WHAT

MATH TEST MISCHIEF

Book design by Jake Slavik
Illustrations by Courtney Huddleston

Design Elements: Shutterstock Images

Published in the United States by Jolly Fish Press, an imprint of North Star Editions, Inc.

First Edition
First Printing, 2019

This is a work of fiction. Names, characters, places, and incidents are either the product of the author's imagination or are used fictitiously, and any resemblance to actual persons living or dead, business establishments, events, or locales is entirely coincidental.

Library of Congress Cataloging-in-Publication Data
Names: Weaver, Verity, author. | Huddleston, Courtney, illustrator.
Title: Math test mischief / by Verity Weaver ; illustrated by Courtney Huddleston.
Description: First edition. | Mendota Heights, MN : Jolly Fish Press, [2020] | Summary: "Every test from Miss Palermo's first period math class is missing, and the students each have their own theory as to what happened"—Provided by publisher.
Identifiers: LCCN 2019001869 (print) | LCCN 2019004536 (ebook) | ISBN 9781631633133 (ebook) | ISBN 9781631633126 (pbk.) | ISBN 9781631633119 (hardcover)
Subjects: | CYAC: Examinations—Fiction. | Lost and found possessions—Fiction. | Schools—Fiction. | LCGFT: Fiction.
Classification: LCC PZ7.1.W41777 (ebook) | LCC PZ7.1.W41777 Mat 2019 (print) | DDC [Fic]—dc23
LC record available at https://lccn.loc.gov/2019001869

Jolly Fish Press
North Star Editions, Inc.
2297 Waters Drive
Mendota Heights, MN 55120
www.jollyfishpress.com

Printed in the United States of America

WHAT HAPPENED?

MATH TEST MISCHIEF

by VERITY WEAVER

illustrated by COURTNEY HUDDLESTON

text by REBECCA J. ALLEN

JOLLY
FiSH
PRESS
Mendota Heights, Minnesota

Chapter 1

Monday, April 1, 7:25 a.m.

April 1 was the most hazardous day of the school year at Harwington Middle School and by far Mei's least favorite date on the calendar. She'd have willingly accepted a cough and stuffed-up nose to stay home in bed. Yet here she was, walking in the school's front door.

"Mei! Mei, check this out!" Amir called from the other side of the lobby.

"Aiya," Mei muttered under her breath. She walked faster, pretending she hadn't heard him. Amir had some dumb prank or joke ready *every* day. The pranks got bigger and more obnoxious on April Fools' Day. Mei wanted to skip whatever "hilarious" gag he had waiting for her. If she could just make it to Miss Palermo's math classroom, the teacher's presence might save her.

Amir took a running leap, landing loudly as his sneakers slapped the tile floor right in front of her. He spread his arms wide, veering left as she tried to dodge him on that side. But that was a fake. Mei spun right, shooting past Amir and down the hall. It was the same move she used to beat defenders on the lacrosse field. Worked every time.

"You're missing out!" Amir called after her.

"So immature," Mei grumbled as she continued on her way to homeroom. There must be a rule against pranks in the Student Code of Conduct. If there wasn't, there should be. She made a mental note to check.

Amir turned and scouted the lobby for someone more appreciative of his talents. His eyes landed on Trinidad's bouncy curls. Trinidad herself wasn't visible over the head of whoever she was talking to, but her hair had a good couple inches on the rest of her. If that weren't enough of a giveaway, there was also her cute best friend, Claudia, standing nearby. He made his way toward them, dodging people heading to class and other pranksters on the way.

"Happy April Fools' Day!" he shouted when he reached the girls, giving them a toothy grin.

Claudia frowned. "You don't wish people a *happy* April Fools' Day, Amir. That's not a thing. Not like someone's birthday, or New Year's Day, or even Valentine's Day."

Trinidad saw her best friend's lips press into a thin line and was sure she knew the words Claudia would say if they weren't too rude: "*Go away.*"

Poor Amir! He really seemed to like Claudia, and Claudia just didn't like him back. He was cute enough, with warm, brown skin and large, happy eyes. If he'd quit the jokes he'd be all right. But he didn't. Ever.

It made the situation awkward. Claudia didn't give Amir any openings, so he talked to Trinidad as an excuse to hang around Claudia. But today, Trinidad really wanted to talk to *Niles*. He'd organized a group to go to the movies last Friday night and had asked Trinidad to sit next to him. The outing had ended up being a disaster. Still, she could smooth things over, but *not* if Niles thought Trinidad was interested in Amir. *What a mess.*

"Happy April Fools' Day, Amir," Trinidad said kindly. She turned back to the conversation she'd been having with Niles.

But Amir didn't take the hint. "I've got this great trick to show you," he said.

Oblivious, Trinidad thought, but she smiled, unable to be rude even if Amir's jokes drove her best friend nuts and risked messing up things with super-cute Niles. Just that little bit of encouragement made Amir's grin grow so big his eyes got squinty.

"A trick? Let's see it then," Niles said. He'd had been chatting up Trinidad, trying to make up for the colossal dunce he'd made of himself at the cinema, when Amir interrupted. As Niles turned to face Amir, he slid closer to Trinidad. Really close, almost knocking elbows. He hoped Amir would buzz off. And that Trinidad wasn't about to shove him away. After the mess last Friday, he couldn't take another monumental embarrassment.

"Watch closely." Amir loved an audience. He played up his preparations, cracking his knuckles, even stretching his neck to one side, then the other. He shook his hands loose and said, "Okay, I'm ready."

He twisted his right arm with his left hand.

But something went terribly wrong.

He shouted, "Ouch!" and his wrist went limp. His eyes grew so wide the whites showed all the way around his pupils. The enormous crack of his wrist breaking startled several other students chatting around them. His gasp of pain drew more eyes. Soon everyone was staring.

"Oh, oh, oh," Trinidad cooed, her hands going out to Amir's wrist, which was bent at a painful-looking angle. Her hands hung there on either side of the injury. She wanted to do something

to make it better but was deathly afraid she might do something wrong and make it worse.

Claudia shouted at their stunned classmates, "Get Nurse Travers! She'll know what to do."

Tears were about to overflow Trinidad's big, brown eyes. "Just breathe—"

"Dude," Niles muttered.

Amir sucked in a sad little sniff like he was trying his best not to cry.

"*Dude*," Niles said more aggressively.

Amir's bottom lip quivered.

Niles's eyes narrowed, and he aimed a punch at Amir's chin, pulling short just before it connected.

Trinidad shrieked.

Amir's hands went up to protect his face. Both of them.

And suddenly, Amir's wrist wasn't bent at an odd angle any longer. A fractured plastic cup fell out from under his armpit and hit the floor with a *crack* that sounded distinctly like the one Amir's wrist had made when it "broke."

"That was complete rubbish." Niles pinned an annoyed look on Amir for a moment, before turning to Trinidad.

Her eyes were enormous. They went from Amir's wrist, now clearly fine, to Niles and back. "You scared me to death!" she said to Amir.

Then she turned to Niles. "And you! What if it wasn't a prank? You didn't know it was a prank!"

Niles's fair skin shaded pink.

Trinidad took off down the hall before either boy could explain or defend himself.

Claudia whacked Amir on the arm. "Idiot!" Then she took off after Trinidad.

Amir snorted as he watched the girls storm off. "That was awesome! Just like I practiced in the mirror. They'll be laughing about it by second period."

"I did not need that today." Niles's tone was still irritated, even more so than it had been a moment ago.

"What?" Amir asked. "The movies didn't go so well?"

Amir hadn't been invited, but he'd heard about the movie plans. Niles, with his "posh" British accent, had been the subject of whispers since he'd moved to Harwington last year. But the rumors had really taken off last week as everyone had tried to sort out who'd been invited and who hadn't, and what it all meant in terms of who liked who.

Niles's flush deepened, making Amir think he'd hit a sore point. What could've gone wrong? Niles was practically Mr. Perfect.

"It went fine, thank you very much." Niles wasn't about to

admit how un-fine things had gone to Amir. "But now, thanks to you, Trinidad's annoyed with me." He stalked off down the hall.

"At least my prank was original!" Amir called after him. Most of the other pranksters scattered around the lobby had stolen gag ideas from last year. Didn't they get that no one was going to fall for white-toothpaste-filled-Oreos two years in a row? You could get the sixth graders with an old joke, but there wasn't much challenge in that.

Amir was in no hurry to get to homeroom while everyone was still annoyed with him. He might as well have a few more minutes of fun until the first bell rang. Tossing the broken plastic cup into the nearest garbage bin, he pulled a new one out of his backpack and tucked it up under his armpit. He tugged his jacket closed to hide it from view. Then he scanned the crowd for a new audience.

All the other eighth graders milling around him had just seen the gag. With the excitement over, they'd turned back to their conversations without so much as a fist bump for Amir's stellar performance.

He started toward the hallway with the sixth graders' lockers. Pulling a gag on sixth graders might score lower on the difficulty scale, but at least he'd get one more good laugh before the school day started.

7:35 a.m.

"Good morning, Miss Palermo," Trinidad said brightly as she and Claudia walked into the math classroom. They had both homeroom and first-period pre-algebra with Miss Palermo, as well as lacrosse practice or games three afternoons a week. Miss Palermo was their coach.

Trinidad hovered just inside the door next to the teacher's desk, but the teacher said, "Good morning, girls," without turning from the problem she was writing on the whiteboard.

Trinidad tossed her long, curly hair over her shoulder and headed down the aisle. She slipped into her seat in the third row with a nod to Mei in the desk behind hers. Then she leaned toward Claudia in the desk on her left and said in a low voice, "I think I overreacted."

"No way. That was *not* funny. The way Amir's wrist was bent, I was sure he'd be stuffed into an ambulance and heading at top speed for emergency surgery."

"Right? It looked so real! And the cup snapping sounded just like a bone breaking." Trinidad shivered.

Niles took his seat at the desk to Trinidad's right. "It did look real, but it was Amir, and today is April Fools' Day. You had to expect something dodgy."

Mei silently congratulated herself for having escaped Amir's stupid trick. She continued reading through Harwington Middle School's Code of Conduct, having downloaded it to her phone from the website. She hadn't found any rules about pranks specifically, but she thought it might fall under the section "Behavior that Could Harm Yourself or Other Students." She marked the page with an electronic bookmark.

Niles pulled out his math notebook and flipped some pages to look busy. He generally spent math class trying to think of things to say to Trinidad—anything to give him an excuse to look at her beautiful face without seeming desperate and pathetic—but right now, his mind was a black hole. Anything he said would only make things worse.

Talking to her should have been easier today. That was the whole idea behind organizing Friday's trip to the cinema, but his brilliant plan had failed miserably. Niles had dropped his soda when an action scene startled him, drenching one of Trinidad's legs with cold, sticky Coke and leaving her jeans sopping wet for the second hour of the movie. Niles had wanted to melt into liquid and slide along the popcorn-littered floor with the Coke. Instead, he'd sat next to Trinidad for the rest of the film, feeling too stupid to even hold her hand.

It hadn't been *a bit* of Coke he'd spilled either. He'd splurged to buy the bladder buster. The only thing that soda had busted was his shot at a date for the semiformal dance next month.

And now, Amir's stunt had Trinidad even more annoyed with him.

"But what if he *had* broken his arm, Niles?" Trinidad asked. "Wouldn't you have felt awful for pretending to punch him?"

"Sure," Niles grumbled. He didn't really think it was possible to break your wrist just by twisting it, not unless you were Dwayne "The Rock" Johnson or the guy who played the Hulk. But telling Trinidad that was not going to help his situation. He needed to let the whole prank thing die down and wait to bring up a second trip to the cinema until tomorrow.

Mei spoke up from the row behind them. "I hope high school kids don't treat April 1 like it's a national holiday, the way people do here. Do they, Miss Palermo?"

"I'm sorry. Does who do what?" The teacher still hadn't turned from the whiteboard, which was now covered top to bottom with formulas. She wasn't cutting them any slack after Friday's test. Instead, she seemed ready to launch full speed into new material.

"Do people in high school pretend to break their wrists, glue the loose end of the toilet paper roll so you can't unroll it, and pull other stupid pranks?" Mei asked. She noticed Amir at the door just as she asked her question and could feel the snarky grin he aimed at her.

Amir shuffled across the classroom and took his seat next to Niles.

Miss Palermo finally finished at the whiteboard and crossed the front of the room to her desk. "No. No, I don't think so. High school students have plenty on their mind in the spring. Exams, prom, graduation." As she said this, she started moving the books and papers on her desk around like she was looking for something.

"Actually," she continued as she pulled open her file drawer and started flipping through files, "that doesn't really sound too different from eighth grade, does it?"

Mei pursed her lips as she thought about that wishy-washy answer. She'd really hoped that high school *was* different from eighth grade. Eighth graders seemed to have plenty of time for pranks, despite the upcoming exams, dance, and graduation.

The students watched Miss Palermo for a moment, hoping she might tell them more about high school. With spring's arrival, the end of eighth grade and their transition to the new school suddenly seemed much closer than it had in the dead of winter. High school felt like a much bigger transition than the one they'd made from elementary school to Harwington Middle, and they wouldn't have minded some advice. But Miss Palermo said nothing more. The blue streak in her white-blonde hair hung down, hiding her face as she rifled through her bag, then through the file drawer again.

Normally, a question about high school would have gotten Miss Palermo chatting. This was her first year teaching, and she was much younger than most of their other teachers. She loved to help her students prepare for future academic success. But today, she seemed distracted. She stood next to her desk, her arms crossed, scanning the room though not really seeing the students sitting there. She looked as un-Miss-Palermo-ish as they'd ever seen her.

"Miss Palermo, is something wrong?" Trinidad asked.

The teacher tugged her chin-length blonde-blue hair with both hands, a sure sign that whatever was bothering her was something serious. "Has anyone seen the pre-algebra tests?" she asked. "They were right here on my desk. I graded them over the weekend and wanted to hand them back, but they've disappeared."

Mei let out a small gasp.

"Someone probably stole them as an April Fools' joke." Niles looked pointedly at Amir.

Amir put his hands up, proclaiming innocence. "Not me, man. I wouldn't want to take a math test a *second* time."

"We won't have to take the test a second time as long as Miss Palermo recorded the grades," Mei said.

"Did you record the grades, Miss Palermo?" asked Amir. "Please tell me you did."

Miss Palermo's head, along with the hands still clutching her hair, shook slowly from side to side. She drew in a deep breath and turned her lips up in a pained-looking smile. "I'm sure the tests will turn up."

"And if they don't?" Mei asked.

"Then I'm afraid everyone will have to study the material again tonight. We'll retake the test tomorrow."

The entire class groaned.

Chapter 2

Mei, 7:40 a.m.

This. Could not. Be happening.

I pulled out my phone and tapped open the text message app. Okay, yes, phones were supposed to be off and away during class, but this was clearly an emergency!

Mama was on the board of the parent-teacher association. She'd have a thing or two to say about missing tests.

Me: Miss Palermo lost the pre-algebra tests. How could a teacher do that? And I studied so hard! I'm sure I aced it! What if I don't do as well when we retake it? It won't be fair!

The three dots appeared immediately. Mama was always on top of anything that had to do with grades.

Mama: I knew it was a bad idea to let you take math with a brand-new teacher. Mrs. Antwerp has been teaching at Harwington Middle for twenty years. She would never lose tests! I know you wanted to take art, Mei, but this is what happens when you don't listen to my advice.

What? Mama was acting like it was *my* fault the tests were lost. That was even more unfair than having to retake a test I'd already aced! No teacher, not even a new teacher, should lose a whole class's worth of tests!

Sorry, Mama. I clicked off my phone's display and placed it facedown on my desk, ignoring it as it vibrated again and again. It radiated disapproval at me. I knew I should obey my elders, especially Mama, but if she wasn't going to help, I needed to think.

I raised my hand, but Miss Palermo didn't see it. She was searching frantically through the supply cabinet, as if anyone would put a stack of tests in there.

"Miss Palermo," I said.

She turned. "Yes, Mei."

"Maybe you left the tests at home. You could run to your

place over lunch and check, then we wouldn't have to study again for nothing."

Miss Palermo shook her head slowly, shut the door to the supply cabinet, and turned to face the class. "I'm sure I brought them in. I was so proud of how well you all did on the challenging material in the last chapter, and I was excited to share the results with you."

She walked to the corner of her desk nearest the classroom door, the chunky heels of her shoes clicking against the floor tiles. "I thought I put the tests right here, like I always do. I don't know where they could have gone."

The corner of the desk right by the door was the worst place to put a pile of tests. Anyone could have swiped them as they walked into the classroom or walked down the hall. It's not like people were watching out for test thieves at 7:30 a.m.

"Did you stop in the teachers' lounge on your way in?" Trinidad asked. "Maybe you just planned to put the tests on the desk like you always do, but you actually left them next to the coffee pot."

Miss Palermo waved absentmindedly at her desk. "No coffee this morning. I was running late." An extra-large green mug that read, "I'm a teacher. What's your superpower?" usually sat at the edge of the desk nearest the whiteboard so Miss Palermo could take a quick sip while the students worked out a problem on their own. The mug was missing today.

"My dad would say lack of caffeine is your problem. He doesn't do anything but grunt until he's on his second cup." Suddenly, Niles sat up straight. "Maybe if I get you some, you'll remember where you left the tests."

He seemed awfully eager to run to the teachers' lounge. That was a bit suspicious.

"Maybe you left them in your car," Amir suggested. "If you have one of those key fobs that beeps when you unlock the doors, I could run to the parking lot and check for you. I'd do anything to not have to study math again tonight."

Now a second boy was looking for an excuse to run out of the classroom! My arms tingled with something that I would call a "Spidey sense" if I read comic books.

Like Niles had said, today was April Fools' Day, and Amir was a prank waiting to happen. He could have taken the tests as a hoax. It was a mean hoax, but no more so than several things I'd seen in the lobby this morning. That was the problem with pranks—they were always gross, embarrassing, or scary. Principal Alvero should really put a stop to them.

But Amir didn't look guilty. With his brows knit and one leg jiggling under his desk, he looked genuinely upset about the prospect of added math work. He could be faking it to throw off suspicion, except he wasn't that good an actor. If I'd seen him fake-break his wrist, I'd have known it was a gag right away.

Someone else could have thought stealing the math tests was funny. I looked from face to face around the room.

In the front row, Lexie pushed up her glasses as she read through her textbook. Lexie never struggled in math. She was probably teaching herself the next chapter now just because there was nothing better to do. Someone who regularly scored 99s on math tests could pull a prank like this. She wouldn't get how much it might upset people who didn't always get As.

Still, Lexie was the quiet type. She cringed anytime Miss Palermo raised her voice to get the class to simmer down. She wouldn't risk getting caught with stolen tests. That turned my attention to Trinidad.

Trinidad sat in the middle of the math classroom like she was the sun and the whole room revolved around her. Niles, to her right, was always turning her way for no clear reason. Claudia, to her left, checked every math problem she did with her. Miss Palermo loved Trinidad too. Trinidad's hand was always up with the answer to a question, and Miss Palermo called on her a ton. She probably got extra class participation credit. It wasn't fair.

Last year, I'd beaten Trinidad on every math test but one. Since we started with Miss Palermo this year, Trinidad's grades were right up there with Lexie's, while I struggled to get high Bs.

She'd have no trouble with taking the test a second time. Plus, Trinidad had spunk. She was loud on the lacrosse field, always calling for the ball, and loud at school. She and Claudia were always getting into other peoples' business. Trinidad pretended she asked about classmates because she cared, but did she?

I didn't think so. I thought she had an agenda. She'd succeeded in getting elected captain of the lacrosse team by kissing up to our teammates. Then she'd used her position as captain to steal the starting attack position from me. Now she was stealing tests.

My non-Spidey sense tingled, making me shiver. Everything fit together—even the look on Trinidad's face. She seemed . . . happy. She was leaning across the aisle toward Claudia in whispered conversation. I couldn't quite make out what they were saying, but they spoke in rushed, squeaky-high tones, not grumbles.

Why would anyone be happy about missing math tests? I leaned closer.

"That test was the worst, and now I get another chance to study!" Trinidad whispered.

Claudia grinned. "Was it the test? Or the fact that your mind was on something other than studying Thursday night?"

Trinidad blew a stray curl off her face. Her eyes shot over to Niles as if to see if he'd heard that comment. He gave no indication that he had.

"I studied," she said defensively.

"Sure. After trying on every possible outfit in your closet."
Claudia glanced up at the front of the room, but Miss Palermo
was still searching for the tests. Claudia pulled up the text app
on her phone. It was full of pictures of Trinidad. "This one, for
example. Or this one."

I caught a glimpse of the images. Trinidad in skinny jeans and
a fuchsia T-shirt. Trinidad in a mini-skirt and leggings. Trinidad
in a bright-white shirt with shoulder cutouts that contrasted with
her brown skin. What the heck was the fashion show about?

Trinidad's eyes went wide, and she shifted, blocking the phone from view. "He'll see," she hissed.

Claudia giggled.

"I was good," Trinidad whispered. "One practice problem, one outfit."

"Then you should've had no problem with the test. I've got pictures of a dozen different outfits here." Claudia waved her phone.

Trinidad made a grab for it but missed. "I don't own a dozen outfits, but I admit I should have studied more. I'm not crying about those missing tests."

Not crying?

Or responsible for the fact that they disappeared and just not admitting it?

That was it. This had nothing to do with April Fools' Day. That was just a convenient distraction from the real issue. Trinidad had stolen the tests because she needed to fix her mistake. She'd been more focused on clothes than her grades, and now the entire class would have to pay for it. She'd even hung out at Miss Palermo's desk when she and Claudia first came into the room. I wished I'd paid more attention to what she was doing up there. But I could guess.

I needed proof that Trinidad had done it. That'd get the retest canceled. It'd also get Trinidad benched. Miss Palermo always said classwork came before sports.

When Trinidad got benched, I'd slide back into the starting attack position and prove I was the better girl for that spot.

I was just about to raise my hand and turn the thief in when Miss Palermo said, "I don't want to accuse anyone of taking those tests. If it was just an April Fools' joke, I'm willing to let it slide, but I need them back." Her gaze rested on each of us for a second before it moved on. The classroom was silent and filled with tension.

I froze. I didn't want to force Trinidad to turn the tests in now when she'd be off the hook. I'd wait until later, then make sure she was caught red-handed.

I had a mission.

Chapter 3

Mei, 7:45 a.m.

Miss Palermo finally took attendance, rushing through the names on the sheet she had to send to the front office. She finished just as the bell signaling the end of homeroom rang.

"Let's put the bad news behind us for the moment and open our books to chapter twelve," she said by way of transition to pre-algebra. "We need to start covering the new material even if we have to pause to retake the test tomorrow."

Math was not my favorite class, but somehow, moving on to

a new chapter while still needing to retake the last test made it that much worse. I had to find those tests.

When class ended, my books were already packed in my bag. I got up and pretended to be waiting impatiently for Trinidad to clear the aisle. Actually, I was peeking into her backpack to look for evidence as she put her stuff away.

Claudia, always minding other people's business instead of her own, pushed through the gap between her desk and the one behind it. She got right in my face. "Keep your nose out of other people's things."

It made me wonder if she was in on Trinidad's plan. She could be. She didn't seem any more disappointed that the tests were missing than Trinidad did.

I flipped my hair over my shoulder and gave Claudia an icy look. "I think we should all keep our noses in other people's things today. There are math tests to find."

"I didn't take the math tests," Trinidad said, but she also zipped her bag closed, rather than prove what she said was true.

"Is that right? What about you, Claudia? Neither of you seemed too upset they're missing." If I discovered the tests in Claudia's bag, it wouldn't work out as well for my lacrosse agenda. Claudia was on the team's starting lineup, but on defense, a position I had no interest in playing. I wanted to *make* goals, not block them.

"Come on, Claudia." Trinidad turned and marched out of the classroom with her friend by her side.

I hung back for a second so they wouldn't notice I was following, then threaded quickly through the crowd in the hallway to catch up. I wished I had one of those detective trench coats or some other disguise.

"I'll do so much better this time," I heard Claudia say.

"No texting until we've done twenty practice problems," Trinidad replied.

One of them definitely had those tests. They were both rule breakers!

That was how Trinidad had stolen the starting attack position from me—by breaking the rules. Shouldering other players out of the way, hitting sticks too hard, crossing the restraining line and risking getting us called offsides for having too many players on one side of the field—why did the refs not see that?

"I'm going to stop by my locker before science," Trinidad said as they reached the classroom door. "If I don't make it before the bell, can you tell Mr. Gopal I'll be just one second?"

Aha! The chills running down my arms had built up to midwinter-blizzard strength. Trinidad had the tests and wanted to hide them in her locker! This was my chance to catch her!

"Sure." Claudia turned to the classroom door. As she did, she caught sight of me and did a double take. She shifted her jaw from left to right. "Snooping in people's backpacks isn't enough? You need to eavesdrop too?"

I knew I needed a disguise! But I recovered quickly, nodding at the science classroom door.

"We were just heading in the same direction. But now that I think about it, my backpack is heavy. I'm going to drop some stuff off at my locker."

Trinidad frowned, not heading down the hall even though time between classes was tight—yet another clue that she planned to drop off the stolen tests. Of course, she couldn't do that with me following.

"Oh no, you're coming with me," Claudia said. "Accusing Trinidad of stealing the tests is one thing. Tailing her around school like a spy is another." She grabbed me by the arm and dragged me into the science classroom.

"Mr. Gopal!" I shrieked, but by the time he looked up from the worksheets he was placing on everyone's desks, Claudia had dropped my arm and was smiling innocently.

Mr. Gopal tipped his head to one side. "Is there a problem, Mei?"

"Yeah, is there a problem, Mei?" Claudia mimicked. As she did, she stepped between me and the door. I faked right and spun left to get around her, but instead, I bounced right into her chest. The collision sent me crashing into the desk behind me. The corner of the chair's back bit into my hip and stung.

"Yeah, I was there the day Miss Palermo had us practice fakes." Claudia's grin was smug.

Aiya! The dodge that had worked so well against Amir was completely useless against other lacrosse players!

"Back off," I said.

"Ladies, the bell is about to ring. Mei, please feed Rattatat. Claudia, please take your seat." Mr. Gopal went back to passing out worksheets, but his gaze kept returning to us.

"Gross! I don't want to feed the rat. You do it, Claudia."

Claudia didn't move. She just lifted an eyebrow, blocking my path to the door. "Rattatat's not gross. He's furry and adorable. And I'm not taking your job just so you can go spy on Trinidad."

There were plenty of people I could have gotten past, but the lacrosse team's starting center defenseman was not one of them. Plus, I didn't want to get in trouble with Mr. Gopal. So I stalked over to the counter where equipment and supplies for lab projects were stored. The rat's cage was also there. I peered through the wire.

How had Mr. Gopal gotten permission to keep a rat as class pet? Rats carried all sorts of germs and diseases. I didn't want to put my hand anywhere near it.

"You're not going to let Rattatat starve, are you?"

I heard the taunt in Claudia's words. Most of my classmates would've been happy to feed the rat. They *liked* it, though I couldn't see why. Why was I stuck feeding it?

The rat was sleeping, as usual, and not likely to jump up and bite me. That made the risk of infection low. I decided to get it over with. Besides, by now the tests were in Trinidad's locker and locked up tight. How could I get to them now?

I shot a scowl at Claudia, then poured several of the smelly pellets from the rat's food bag into my hand. Then I froze.

Right next to the cage and rat food were the simple stethoscopes we'd made out of funnels and balloons one day. We'd cut the elastic material of the balloon in half and stretched it across the wide end of the funnel, then taped it in place. With our ears to the narrow end of the funnels, we'd used these "stethoscopes" to measure each other's heart rates at rest and after a minute of jogging in place to see how much exercise elevated them.

Stethoscopes.

Just like crooks in heist movies used to crack safes.

It would be a whole lot easier to break the code on the little combination lock on Trinidad's locker than to crack a safe, and those stethoscopes were powerful enough to make a heartbeat audible. They'd work!

There was only one problem: breaking into someone's locker was definitely against the rules. I didn't need to check the Student Code of Conduct. I knew it was wrong. A tight feeling tugged at my chest.

Still, it was Trinidad who should feel guilty, not me. She stole the tests. My rule-breaking was needed to fix Trinidad's greater rule-breaking. Breaking into her locker would set things right.

With that realization, the tightness rushed out of my chest like air escaping a balloon.

The bell rang.

Trinidad came sprinting into the room looking sweaty and guilty.

I pried open the lid on the cage a smidge, dropped in the food pellets, and shoved the lid back down tight. Then I swiped one of the stethoscopes, tucking it between my arm and my side where it wouldn't be obvious to Claudia or any other busybodies.

Walking back to my seat, I decided I'd need a trip to the girl's room halfway through class.

Chapter 4

Mei, 9:05 a.m.

I didn't think of one critical problem with my plan until I was out of the classroom, holding the bathroom pass in one hand and the handmade stethoscope in the other.

I had no idea what Trinidad's locker number was.

That didn't stop me though. I'd come too far to turn back now. That sounded like the lyrics of some pop song, maybe something Selena Sanchez would sing. I imagined Selena belting out that line to a stadium jam-packed with dancing fans, just like I imagined myself leading the Harwington Middle School lacrosse team to victory to the cheers of supporters. *I've come too far to turn back now.*

Locate Trinidad's locker.

Find the evidence to get that rule breaker convicted of her crime.

Step into my rightful spot as the lacrosse team's starting attacker.

I imagined a drumbeat for my theme song and tapped it out on the stethoscope's elastic end as I strode to the hall with the eighth-grade lockers. The sound twanged through the silent corridor. I puzzled through the locker-number problem as I went.

Think. Think, I told my brain. There was a way to solve this.

Ask the ladies in the front office for Trinidad's locker number? No. They'd see through any excuse I made up for why I needed it.

Call Mama and wheedle her into getting the number from the office? No. She'd ask a million questions and probably blame me for the situation I was in *again*.

Break into all 200 eighth-grade lockers? Obviously not. I didn't have all day.

There had to be a way. *I've come too far to turn back now.*

Then I had it. Picturegram. Everyone used that app to share their selfies and other photos. I shoved the bathroom pass into my back pocket and pulled out my phone, tapping its screen to open the app. Then I looked up Trinidad's account. We'd followed each other last year, before the lacrosse lineup got competitive.

I stopped when I found the picture I was looking for. First day of school. Trinidad and Claudia decorating lockers. There were photos of them standing at two different lockers. One was decorated with lacrosse stickers, posters of a boy band, and a pink-framed mirror. Definitely Claudia's locker.

In the next selfie, they were standing next to a locker decorated with lacrosse stickers, a picture of Trinidad in her lacrosse gear, and a picture of a woman who could only be her mother. This was Trinidad's locker.

Since the locker door was open, I couldn't see the number, but the locker next to it was 554. That meant Trinidad's locker was number 553. I had her.

I found the right locker, shoved my phone back into my pocket, and grabbed the lock—just as Niles came around the corner.

Aiya! Niles might know which locker was Trinidad's. I couldn't let him catch me breaking into it.

"Ugh, wrong locker," I muttered and headed down the row of lockers toward my own. I pretended to be busy opening my own combination lock and looking through my textbooks.

Niles's eyebrows went up as he passed me, but he didn't say anything. Maybe he didn't know Trinidad's locker number.

When he turned the corner, I heaved a sigh of relief, went straight back to locker 553, and set to work breaking in.

Chapter 5

Trinidad, 9:30 a.m.

I pushed my science notebook away after class ended, glad I could finally tell Claudia the news that had been bothering me all period.

"Miss Palermo's in trouble. When I went to my locker before class, I saw her talking with Principal Alvero in the hall. She looked so . . . I don't know . . . sad? Embarrassed? It must be the worst to be a new teacher and have tests disappear."

Claudia slid her backpack onto one shoulder. "Sure, it stinks, but it's not your problem. What can you do about it?" She started toward the door.

I kept up, knocking shoulders with her as we headed down the hall to our third-period rooms. "Don't you mean what can *we* do about it? We need to find those tests!"

"Um, no." Claudia shook her finger left to right. "Because *we* have this super plan for fixing our texting-more-than-studying mistake, remember? We both need to retake that test and do well."

I winced. "That test you got a D on was two months ago. Is your mom still on your case about it?"

"Yes. One more test under a B, and I'm getting 'help.' This help conflicts with lacrosse practice, so this is not something to fool around about."

I bit the inside of my cheek. "You're right. I need to keep my math grades up if I want to get into the STEM magnet school."

"'If'?" Claudia waved at a couple girls heading down the hall in the opposite direction, then went on. "Don't get me wrong. I'd rather you didn't go hang with the nerds, since there's no way I'm getting into that high school, but I didn't really think it was an *if* for you."

I peeked over at Claudia, gauging her expression. It was awkward talking with her about the magnet school because until this year, we'd expected to go to high school together and take as many of the same classes as we could. We'd play lacrosse together.

We'd keep trying on too many outfits before meet-ups with boys, though hopefully without messing up our grades in the process next time. The thought of going to an academically tough school without her by my side was like heading up the first big hill on a roller coaster: There'd be some awesome in my future, but it would come with fear, shrieks, and nausea.

But the magnet school was an opportunity I had to try for. Miss Palermo had shown me I could be good at math and that there were cool things I could do if I kept my grades up. Coding. Engineering.

There were classes at the magnet school that sounded amazing. I could learn to do video editing, animate video-game characters, or design things and print them out on 3-D printers. The thought that I'd be able to do stuff like that kind of blew my mind. I couldn't say I knew what I wanted to do when I "grew up," but Mom always talked about the importance of education and how it gave you options for the future.

That was why getting into the STEM school was so important. Options.

Claudia didn't look sad or accusing. She wanted me to have options, too, even if that meant we'd be at different schools next year. She was an awesome best friend.

"Okay," I said. "I need to keep my math grade up *because* I want to get into the STEM school. But how can I not help Miss

Palermo? I wouldn't have had a shot at getting in without her help and the great recommendation she wrote."

"That's just it. Miss Palermo really wants to see you get in, so you need to retake that test." Claudia crossed the hall and stopped at her locker. "Hold up a sec while I grab my music." She spun the dial on the combination lock.

I propped my back against the next locker over. "She does want me to get in. It just doesn't seem fair that Miss Palermo should get in trouble for a problem someone else caused."

I watched my classmates as they walked down the hall. Mei had this irritated look on her face. There was definitely something up with her today. Others were still pulling April Fools' pranks. A guy dropped a fake cockroach down the back of another boy's shirt. A couple girls giggled as they pressed buttons on a fart machine.

Where there'd been shrieks at the start of the day, now there was just laughter. News of who was pulling which gags had made it around the school, and also, everyone was suspicious. Guards were up. Unfortunately, Miss Palermo's guard hadn't been up at the start of the school day when it mattered.

I thought back through homeroom and the start of first period when she'd discovered the tests were missing. "The thief must be someone in pre-algebra with us. Miss Palermo was at the whiteboard the whole time people were walking in. With the tests right there on her desk, it could have been anyone."

Claudia slammed her locker shut and relocked it. We started down the hall toward the auditorium where I had theater. She'd head to the choir room.

"You stopped at her desk for a second. Were the tests there?" she asked.

I shrugged. "I looked, 'cause my stomach was doing somersaults about my grade and whether I was disappointing her, but I didn't see them."

Claudia's brows furrowed. "Maybe someone swiped them before homeroom started."

"Someone who loves April Fools' Day," I said, building on her thought. "Who always has a big prank up his sleeve. Someone who might've come in early today just to play a trick like this."

"Amir," we both said at the same time.

"Pretending to break a wrist was a decent gag," Claudia said. "But not even close to what he did last year."

We walked in silence for a moment. "It was kind of suspicious—the way Amir wanted to go out and check in Miss Palermo's car," I said finally.

"Like maybe he had the tests and wanted to plant them someplace where she could find them later."

We reached the auditorium, and I stopped. "But if he borrowed Miss Palermo's car keys 'to look for the tests,' then she'd know it was him when the tests turned up there."

"Ah." Claudia brought up one index finger. "But if he stashed them there, but not someplace obvious, he could say he hadn't seen them. Miss Palermo wouldn't be able to prove she hadn't forgotten them there herself. Plus, he'd have had us all going with his prank for at least half a day. Miss Palermo has classes back-to-back all morning. She wouldn't have a chance to check until lunch."

"Amir loves tricking people. He was beaming about convincing us he'd broken his wrist for sixty seconds—"

"—and he didn't really even trick Niles."

"So having the whole pre-algebra class plus Miss Palermo searching for the tests for hours—"

"—would make his day."

"His *year*."

"I can already hear him bragging it was the best April Fools' Day prank Harwington Middle School ever saw. 'The infamous day the tests disappeared.' "

I tried to imagine Amir thinking he could pull off something like that. It did feel like an Amir prank. "If he came in early and snatched the tests, he could have hidden them in his backpack and then come back to the lobby to pull the wrist-breaking prank as an alibi."

Claudia nodded. "Now he's stuck with them in his bag and nervous about it. That's why he offered to go to her car. Lunch is his first chance to sneak them back into the classroom without Miss Palermo catching him."

"There's just one problem," I said. "He seemed genuinely upset about retaking the test."

Claudia rolled her eyes. "He also seemed like he'd for-real broken his wrist."

I nodded, convinced. "We need to tell him that he's taken this gag too far and needs to give the tests back now. He's in choir with you this period, right?"

Claudia nodded.

"Bring him to the theater after class. Center stage. I have a plan."

Claudia smiled, then spun on her heel and headed down the hall.

Chapter 6

Trinidad, 10:25 a.m.

By the time Claudia and Amir arrived, I was in position at the light board backstage. I watched through the curtains as they walked to center stage.

Amir was scanning the room. "Where is she? We've got to get to English."

I launched my offensive strike. First, I flipped a spotlight on Amir. I knew from experience that he was in the hot seat now.

Those intense lights made you sweat even if you hadn't just stolen a whole bunch of math tests.

Then I hit the microphone so my voice boomed through the whole auditorium. "Return the math tests! Miss Palermo's an awesome teacher. The best."

Amir recovered quickly from his surprise. He squinted and put his hands up to block the light. "She teaches *math*! There is no such thing as an awesome math teacher."

"You can't steal her tests just because she teaches a subject you don't like," Claudia said.

"I don't believe you hate math so much," I added. "I heard you're at the top of Mrs. Jones's computer programming class. Aren't computer programmers good at math?"

"Not in my case."

I walked out from behind the curtains so I could read Amir's expression. Claudia eyed him with suspicion too. Everything seemed to point to Amir: the love for pranks, the motivation to get to school early on April Fools' Day to set up a *big* prank, his offer to run out to her car. He'd even pulled pranks on Miss Palermo before.

"Why'd you want to check her car if you weren't trying to plant the tests there?" I asked, closing in on him.

"Why'd Niles offer to check the teacher's lounge? Because we don't want to take an *extra* math test!"

Claudia was watching him with eagle eyes. "His gaze shifted up and to the left. Is that the direction that means he's lying or telling the truth? I forget what they say on the cop shows."

Amir's hands went out like he was pleading with us to understand. "I'm telling you guys, I didn't do it."

After the acting job he'd done in the lobby, I needed more than innocent gestures and puppy eyes. "Prove it."

His face bunched up around his mouth and forehead. "How can I prove I *didn't* do something? That's impossible. It's not like I've been wearing a GoPro all morning tracking my whereabouts, ready to give you video evidence."

"That's a good idea for next April Fools' Day," Claudia said. "You're a very pranksterish type of guy. A camera would keep you from getting into too much trouble."

Now Amir's hands bounced in the air. "Fun pranks. I do fun pranks. Retaking a math test is *not* fun."

"Scaring us half to death with a broken wrist wasn't fun, either," I said, moving even closer.

Amir winced. "I thought it was. At least, I thought you'd think it was fun after." His eyes were fixed on Claudia's ballet flats as if they were the most interesting things ever.

I tried another approach. "Show us what's in your backpack."

Amir turned to angle his backpack away from me.

Suspicious. *Totally suspicious.* His backpack looked like it was stuffed abnormally full.

"What've you got to hide?" Claudia stepped behind him.

Amir moved toward the edge of the stage, keeping his bag out of reach. "Prank supplies. *Duh.* I don't want any spoilers to leak out."

"We won't tell," Claudia promised, a mischievous smile on her face.

"Stay back!" Amir said, but Claudia stepped closer anyway.

"Miss Palermo's not like Mrs. Antwerp, here for twenty years, long enough a few parents had her." I moved in, too, trying to get an angle on the zipper on Amir's bag. "She could get in serious trouble."

Amir glanced down at his watch. "The bell's about to ring."

Claudia moved to block Amir from taking off. Her eyes were narrowed, no-nonsense, accusing. Claudia in her "not getting past me" defense stance destroyed any hope of him getting away. Sweat broke out on his forehead.

"Come clean," Claudia demanded.

Amir gulped. "Come to the movies with me. A double date, with Trinidad and Mr. Perfect."

Claudia's nose wrinkled up. "Wait, what does going to the movies have to do with Miss Palermo's math tests?"

"Wait, why is Niles 'Mr. Perfect'?" I asked.

"Aha! I knew you liked him! You knew *exactly* who I was talking about." Amir leapt toward me, and I stepped back, right into the spotlight! Now it felt like *I* was the one under interrogation.

"Is it his newly perfectly messy hair you're into? Or the fact that he sounds just like 'Bond, James Bond'?" Amir did a perfect impression of the British spy's famous line.

"I-I . . ." I didn't know what to say. Movie night had been a disaster. I'd tried to smooth it over with Niles this morning, but we'd been interrupted by Amir's prank. Now Niles was acting kind of distant. Plus, I was mad at him about fake punching Amir. Everything was such a mess today. I definitely wasn't ready for rumors that I liked him to be going around.

Amir rubbed his chin thoughtfully. "How long do you think he spends in front of the mirror every morning getting his hair to look perfectly messy? As if his blond hair and blue eyes weren't enough without the hair gel."

"Guys don't spend time on their hair," Claudia said. "Maybe it's just naturally messy."

Amir raised an eyebrow.

"Anyway, what does going to the movies have to do with the math tests?" Claudia asked again.

Now that I thought about it, Niles's hair *was* different lately. Cooler than it had been before winter break.

"What about his reaction to the wrist prank?" Amir went on, stepping toward me. "Last year, he laughed off the toothpaste-filled Oreos. This year, he's all testy because I got him in trouble with you, Trinidad. All of a sudden, he's acting like he needs to be perfect or he's gonna die."

Claudia's index finger went up. "You know, Amir could have a point there."

The idea that Niles might have changed his hair and gotten annoyed about Amir's prank just because of me made my stomach feel like it was full of something bubbly, like ginger ale that'd been shaken up until it was totally fizzy and threatening to explode. I would have to rethink that whole fake-punch situation in light of this new information.

"But that doesn't matter now." Claudia crossed her arms over her chest. "You're distracting us. And no one's going to any movies with a thief."

Amir flushed deeply enough that red colored his light-brown skin. His gaze returned to Claudia's turquoise ballet flats.

Claudia rolled her eyes.

And suddenly, I could see the possibility of a deal to be made here. After all, Amir was cute and fun, if you could get past his never-ending supply of tricks. Claudia might have fun at the movies with him. Plus, I'd get another shot at a movie with Niles, hopefully without Coke-soaked jeans this time. But

Claudia and Amir weren't going to get this deal done on their own. I had to help.

"This is perfect, actually," I said. "Here's what we're gonna do. Claudia, you are going to a movie with me next weekend. Saturday evening, not Friday, because of . . . reasons." We'd have plenty of time to decide on outfits without messing up Thursday-night homework this way.

Then I looked pointedly at Amir. "*You* are going to show us what's in your bag. If there are no math tests, then . . . it's a free country. Anyone else might go to the movies on Saturday if they wanted to." This would get him his opportunity, without Claudia having to officially agree to a date. Win-win.

"But I highly suggest there are no pranks at this movie event," I added, the key that might get my best friend to see that Amir was a good guy.

Both Claudia and Amir sputtered—her with incredulity, him with happiness—but there was no time to be diplomatic about this. The first bell rang shrilly from a speaker right over our heads. We only had sixty seconds to get to class.

"Maybe we'll invite Niles too." I hoped my tone was casual, not over-the-top excited about my new insight into Niles.

"Now that that's settled." I poked Amir in the shoulder. "Show us what's in your backpack."

Amir looked to Claudia, his expression skeptical. I had to

admit, the vibe she was sending off was not, "Yay! Movies with Amir!"

It was several long seconds before Claudia said, "I'll go to the movies with you, Trinidad. And I'll sit next to an open seat that could be available to . . . someone else." She backed off from her defensive stance to something more casual.

Amir peeked up from beneath long, dark eyelashes. "Okay, I'll take that deal, but you two have to trust me to find the test thief. I've come up with my best prank ever. It'll help me find the thief, but I need to pull it off anonymously to avoid getting into trouble. I'll report back as soon as I've got the tests!" He dodged Claudia and dashed down the stage steps and out of the auditorium.

Claudia and I looked at each other. She planted her fists on her hips. "I just got scammed into agreeing to a sort-of date, and he didn't even prove he didn't have the tests."

"We both got scammed, but he's in English with us."

"Right. Let's go."

Claudia and I sprinted down the now-empty halls as the piercing sound of the second bell rang out.

Chapter 7

Trinidad, 10:31 a.m.

Claudia and I got the "You're late—make no noise, and I might not send you to the office" glare from Mr. Bradford when we reached English. Amir sat in the back row with his laptop already out on his desk. He was frantically typing, even though Mr. Bradford hadn't really launched into anything worth taking notes on yet.

Claudia looked at him suspiciously as she took her seat a couple rows in front of him. Amir was so focused on his screen he missed it, and he never missed any attention from Claudia. I took my seat in the middle of the room and took out my notebook.

I'd forgotten about Amir's laptop. In fifth grade, he'd switched to typing notes and assignments, rather than handwriting them, because of his sloppy penmanship. Was that laptop the reason his backpack looked overstuffed?

Then again, the laptop meant he didn't need to carry notebooks for every class like the rest of us did. Maybe the folder full of swiped tests still fit. I peered at his bag, trying to estimate how full it was without the laptop, but it was too far across the room for me to tell.

Mr. Bradford launched into his lecture on the act in *Romeo and Juliet* we'd read last night, and I focused back on my own work. I'd already messed up that math test. I didn't want to mess up in English as well.

Anyway, Amir sat in the far back corner of the room. Claudia was in front of him, and I had the easiest access to the door of all three of us. We'd catch him after class and get the answer he'd avoided giving us in the auditorium.

I tried to keep my attention on Mr. Bradford, but it kept getting pulled back to Amir. His thick, dark eyebrows were drawn together in concentration. He continued typing rapidly and clicking his mouse. His eyes were 90 percent on his screen,

10 percent on Mr. Bradford, like he was just pretending to listen to the teacher, rather than actually paying attention.

Also, there were notes to take, sure, but no one needed to type Mei's answer to Mr. Bradford's question on symbolism word for word. I wondered if Amir always took tons of notes and I was just noticing it today, but I didn't think so. Either he was the most detailed notetaker in the history of Harwington Middle School, or he was up to something.

What could he be up to? What could all that clicking and typing have to do with the missing math tests?

Amir caught me glancing his way, waggled his eyebrows at me, and turned his screen so it was angled away from me. Well, I couldn't see before he turned it, but just the fact that he wanted to make sure I couldn't see what he was doing seemed awfully suspicious.

With five minutes left of class, Mr. Bradford let us start reading the next act of the play. Amir finally stopped typing. He couldn't pretend to be taking notes any longer. He rolled his shoulders a couple times like they'd kinked up with all that computer work. He cracked his knuckles, turned his laptop off, and put it back in his bag, putting the bag on the far side of his desk so I *still* couldn't see how full it was.

Read, Trinidad, read. He couldn't get past us.

But just as I found the right page in *Romeo and Juliet*, Amir shouldered his bag—it did look immense, like that laptop, the missing tests, and the textbook for every class we had were in there—and walked toward the teacher's desk.

Claudia looked at me as he passed her. I shrugged. What could we do? Anyway, Mr. Bradford wouldn't let him out early.

Amir stopped at Mr. Bradford's desk and said something to the teacher in a low voice. After a minute of back-and-forth discussion, Mr. Bradford sighed and waved Amir toward the door.

I jumped up. *No! He can't go!*

When my classmates turned around to stare, I realized I'd spoken out loud. I felt like hiding under my desk when Mr. Bradford turned his stern gaze on me.

Amir didn't look at Claudia or me as he slid out of the room a couple minutes before the bell *and* a couple minutes before we could stop him, but I'd swear there was a faint grin on his face.

You wait, Amir. You can't pull that move in every class. I had one more class before lunch, and he wasn't in it. But he couldn't hide all day.

Chapter 8

Amir, 11:18 a.m.

It took some fast-talking to get Mr. Bradford to let me out of English a couple minutes early. I had to upgrade from "I need a bathroom break" to "dangerously close to a smelly mess" to get past his "You can wait two minutes, like everyone else."

I was desperate. Desperate to avoid being interrogated by Claudia and Trinidad *again*. I didn't want to make them mad and mess up my invite to the movies on Saturday. I might not get another shot at that. But I also couldn't get pinned down at the end of class. For my plan to work, I needed to be in social studies super early so I had time to set up my trap for Niles. When I caught him with the math tests, the girls would be so happy to have Miss Palermo off the hook that they'd forget I'd avoided their questions.

Of course, Trinidad wouldn't be happy to find out it was Niles who'd taken the tests, but that was his problem, not mine. My guess was that he'd thought he was helping her by stealing the tests. It was no secret she'd been upset after math on Friday. But he hadn't counted on her friendship with Miss Palermo being more important to her than her math grade.

I made quick progress through the empty hallways, speeding past the bathroom I didn't really need. That bathroom gave me an idea though. The program I needed for my prank was on my flash drive, ready to download and launch, but I still needed a distraction for Mrs. Hasan. The bathroom would work.

The bell signaling the end of fourth period rang just as I got to Mrs. Hasan's classroom. I was at her desk before her fourth-period students were even out of their seats. Perfect timing.

"A girl just ran into the bathroom. She looked sick, like she might need some help." I crossed my fingers behind my back as I told Mrs. Hasan the fib. I wasn't really sure why people thought crossed fingers did anything to offset a lie, but the star of my favorite online prank show always did it, so I figured it couldn't hurt.

"Who?" The gray-haired teacher pushed herself up from her chair. "Which bathroom?"

"The one just down the hall," I said. "I don't know who it was."

"Tell everyone to start the assigned reading if I'm not back before the bell rings." Mrs. Hasan pointed to where she always had the homework written on the whiteboard.

"I will." I watched her leave the room, then got to work.

The SMART board was already on, a slide titled "Critical Battles in the Civil War" displayed on the screen. That eliminated one risk. I'd planned this prank for computer science, because Mrs. Jones always used the SMART board. Mrs. Hasan usually did, but not always. I'd gotten lucky.

On the left side of the system, I found three USB slots. One was already taken. That was the one receiving signals from Mrs. Hasan's wireless mouse and keyboard.

"Sorry, Mrs. Hasan." I pulled out that receiver and put in my own, clicking "Enter" when the option to download the driver for the new device came up on the screen. I slid my flash drive into the next slot down. On my way back to my seat, I stuck Mrs. Hasan's receiver in my pocket.

From my seat at the back of the room, I now controlled the

SMART board. I had my file downloaded to the desktop and Mrs. Hasan's slide back up on the screen before my classmates started trickling into the room. The slideshow presentation covered my new icon. It was hard to keep the smile of satisfaction off my face. This was going to be spectacular!

Just then, Mr. Perfect strutted in with his best friend, Rick, at his side. Did he practice walking like that, long strides, shoulders back, like he didn't have a care in the world? I thought about the way I'd scurried through the halls to get here. Okay, I had been in a hurry and a bit nervous about pulling off this prank, but I didn't think I walked like Niles even on a normal day. Not even when I'd flawlessly pulled off my awesome wrist-break trick this morning. Maybe it wasn't just the perfectly messy hair that got Trinidad and the other girls interested in Niles. Still, I couldn't imagine myself strutting around the school like that. I hoped Claudia didn't go for that type of thing. *Did she?*

Mr. Perfect shot me an annoyed look, like he still blamed me for the fact that Trinidad was mad at him. I scowled back. I hadn't made him fake punch me.

Trinidad and everyone would soon see that he wasn't Mr. Perfect. He was Mr. Test Thief. That would change things.

It was Trinidad herself who had clued me in that Niles had stolen the tests. She'd brought up the fact that I'd wanted to go check for them in Miss Palermo's car. Why did that make me

suspicious? Retaking a math test I'd already taken was worse than having to fight a video-game boss on near-zero health using my backup weapon when I was dying for a bathroom break. *Anyone* would rather find those tests. Mr. Perfect wanted to check the teachers' lounge. But no one accused *him* of stealing the tests.

That's what first got me suspicious of Niles, but it wasn't the only clue. Niles always talked nonstop in pre-algebra, in that accent that somehow made him sound *brilliant* even if he was just complaining about how badly his favorite football team was doing in the World Cup. (*Hello.* They call it *soccer* here!) He'd said this morning that his dad never did anything but grunt until he was on his second cup of coffee. Niles must fill up on coffee, too, because he was always wound up, mostly talking nonstop to Trinidad and Claudia so I couldn't get one word in.

Then, today, he hardly said anything. Like he didn't want to draw attention to himself or the tests he'd slid into his backpack when no one was looking.

I saw through Niles. Trinidad was right about one thing though: Pretending you were upset about the missing tests shifted blame away. Pretending you wanted to search for them would give you an opportunity to stash the tests somewhere else.

I hoped Niles hadn't stashed the tests somewhere between classes. I had no plan for how I'd find them anywhere other than in his bag. Hopefully, I wouldn't have to worry about that. I'd find the tests in his bag and solve the math test mystery this period.

Niles took his seat in the middle of the room. He turned and shot me the evil eye. I ignored him. Soon enough, I'd spring my stunt and he'd be distracted, along with everyone else in the room.

The second bell rang, marking the start of fifth period, and Mrs. Hasan hustled into the room out of breath.

"I couldn't find anyone sick in the girls' room," she said to me.

I cocked my head to one side and recrossed my fingers under my desk. "That's weird. Maybe she went to the nurse's office before you got there."

"Maybe." The teacher pressed her mouth into a flat line for an uncomfortable moment, then she launched into the day's material. "Anyway, I hope everyone is ready for some gripping military strategy, because today, we're talking about the battles that determined the outcome of the Civil War."

I slid my mouse and mouse pad onto my lap so no one could see what I was doing, and I prepared to put my plan into action.

Chapter 9

Amir, 11:25 a.m.

"The Battle of Bull Run was the first major battle . . ."

I waited, letting Mrs. Hasan introduce the topic and giving everyone time to get their notebooks out, put the date on the top of the page, and get their eyes on the SMART board. When attention was focused on the front of the room, I struck.

Mrs. Hasan moved on to the Battle of Shiloh, and I moved my mouse to bring the pointer to the bullet point she was talking about. I spotted Mei sitting in the front of the classroom, furrowing her brow, but Mrs. Hasan, looking out at us, didn't even notice the pointer move. She just went on about why the Battle of Shiloh was important.

I right-clicked and selected highlight mode, then placed a check next to each subpoint as Mrs. Hasan mentioned it.

Now, it wasn't only Mei who'd noticed something odd was going on. A few people were looking from Mrs. Hasan to her hands—which she was waving to emphasize each of her points— to the check marks appearing on the screen.

Mei's hand went up, but Mrs. Hasan said, "Please hold questions until I've given you the overview of the major battles, and then I'd be happy to discuss them in more detail."

Mei shoved her hand under her leg as if that was the only way she could keep it from going back up in the air.

By the time Mrs. Hasan reached the Battle of Antietam, there were puzzled faces all over the room and whispers buzzing through with each new check mark.

The teacher frowned. "There is no need for side conversations."

"But Mrs. Hasan, there's a ghost in your SMART board." Mei said this all in a rush.

Mrs. Hasan looked at Mei like she was an alien with two heads. "A ghost in my SMART board? What on earth—"

"Look!" Mei pointed at the check marks I'd made.

Mrs. Hasan's eyes went wide. She put her hand on her mouse

and moved it in circles. Since I'd unplugged her receiver, the pointer on the screen didn't move, at least until I decided to help her out by underlining some key words on her slide.

Won against overwhelming odds.

Demonstrated that President Lincoln was determined to preserve the Union.

Brought the war to the North.

I kept my arm completely still and moved my wrist the least amount possible, not wanting to give away my identity as the "ghost." When I paused to take in the reactions in the room, I found Niles, turned toward me again, his eyes narrowed to slits.

"What?" I mouthed at him.

He scowled.

His suspicion, and particularly the fact that he couldn't prove it was me messing with the SMART board, made me feel like I'd scored 100 on a math test . . . like I'd asked Claudia to the movies and she'd shouted, "Sure!" and bounced on the balls of her feet in excitement . . . like I'd been named the king of April Fools' Day. This was awesome!

And I was just getting started.

With three quick clicks, I minimized Mrs. Hasan's PowerPoint presentation and launched the program I'd designed to play a prank on Mrs. Jones, my computer-programming teacher. A few small improvements in English class had it ready to use here. It'd give me the perfect opportunity to prove that Niles had stolen the math tests and make sure the rest of us didn't need to take the test again. Operation Cats in History was a go.

My first meme spun as it flew in from the left side of the screen. When it reached the center of the screen, it stopped rotating and grew until it filled the entire SMART board. It showed an enormous picture of a tan shorthaired cat wearing an elaborate gold necklace with a large gem at its center.

Rick read the meme's caption aloud: " 'Cats were considered gods in ancient Egypt. We have not forgotten this.' "

Everyone in the room cracked up, except for Mrs. Hasan. "Who is doing this? Is one of you doing this?" she asked.

I laughed along with my classmates and tried to look as clueless as everyone else.

Next, a black-and-white longhaired cat wearing a white Shakespearean ruff around its neck zoomed in from the right side of the screen. Mei read this caption: "I thumb my nose at thee."

Phones were pulled from pockets and bags. With the growing chaos in the classroom, the "Off and Away" policy was blatantly disregarded. My classmates got busy posting pictures of the cat memes to Picturegram and Snaptalk as fast as they hit the SMART board.

Mrs. Hasan jerked at her mouse a few more times, trying to drag the cursor down to the restart button, but of course,

she couldn't. I'd hijacked the SMART board controls, and I wasn't done with my plan. She picked up the mouse, turned it upside down, switched it off and on, and tried again to reboot the SMART board.

Behind her, the next cat meme featured a cat wearing a medieval chain-mail helm. "I must continue my quest—to slay the red dot," read Niles.

Mrs. Hasan opened the mouse's battery compartment and took the batteries out, then put them back in. She tried her mouse again.

Still no luck.

She peered around the room, likely looking for someone to blame. I was careful to keep the mouse and mouse pad resting on my leg hidden under the desk. I didn't need them any longer—the program would continue to run on its own with a new cat meme flying onto the screen every twenty seconds. But I couldn't put the mouse and mouse pad away without getting caught by Mrs. Hasan, Niles, or other curious eyes.

A gray cat wearing a feathered hat and a button that said "Votes for women" hit the screen.

"Hands. I want to see everyone's hands." Mrs. Hasan waved her own hands in front of her as if to make doubly sure her message was clear.

I felt kind of bad. Mrs. Hasan clearly had no idea what she

was dealing with. The memes were on autopilot. I put my hands in the air along with everyone else, but that didn't stop the cats.

If I'd pulled this prank in computer-programming class as planned, Mrs. Jones would be laughing along with the rest of us by now. She'd be launching into a discussion about how the prank had been programmed. Mrs. Hasan had no idea how to find the culprit or how to stop the memes.

Mrs. Hasan walked up and down the aisles, her hard gaze searching each student intently, like stopping the memes was a matter of life or death. She looked at me, and my breath hitched. It was like being caught in a failed prank. On stage. In front of the entire school. While naked. I was frozen, awaiting her accusation. But after a long, torturous moment, she moved on to Bea in the desk in front of me.

The next meme came up, showing a Himalayan cat wearing an eye patch and a black pirate hat. The caption read: "Ahoy, me hearties! Ready to search for the lost treasure of Blackbeard?"

Chapter 10

Amir, 11:45 a.m.

"Search for lost treasure? Are we going on a field trip?" Rick asked Mrs. Hasan.

The teacher crossed her arms. "I'm sure I don't know. If we are, I hope the ghost in the SMART board ordered us a bus."

On the screen, the next hint came up. Lexie read it: "'The treasure is near, no farther than the door. If you seek to claim it, you must explore!'"

"It's right here in the classroom!" Rick looked around like he was seeing the classroom for the first time ever.

"What could the treasure be?" Bea asked.

"A homework pass?" Mei sat up in her chair.

"Ten extra points on the next test?" Niles peered under his desk.

"I'd take either!" Rick said.

Me too. Mrs. Hasan's reputation for being the toughest social studies teacher in the school was totally valid. Except I knew there was no real treasure, just the distraction I needed for my search.

"Did you hide treasure, Mrs. Hasan?" Mei asked.

"No," Mrs. Hasan said grumpily. "The only treasure in this classroom today was supposed to be knowledge about the major battles of the Civil War."

"Your SMART board isn't working with you on that," Rick said.

The teacher looked like she wanted to argue but couldn't under the circumstances.

Mention of the SMART board drew everyone's eyes back to the screen where the cat memes were now spinning in a circle. The circle drew tighter and tighter, and the memes shrunk in size until they were barely more than a dot in the center of the screen. Then the tiny memes exploded in a violent eruption, forming a cloud of little squares at the top of the screen.

One by one, the squares slowly floated down to the bottom of the screen. As each meme settled, it grew large again and its caption was replaced by a clue.

Mrs. Hasan read the first one. "'Hey there, matey, here's one place you should check: Get off your bottom and down on the deck'?" Her face wrinkled up, hitching her large-framed eyeglasses further up on her nose. "What 'deck'? What does that mean?"

Before she'd even finished reading the clue, half of the students were out of their seats and searching underneath their desks for treasure. When they didn't find anything under their own desks, they started crawling around to look under the other desks near them. This jammed the aisles with students bumping into each other in their haste to be the first to discover . . . something.

During this chaos, I took a moment to slip my mouse pad and mouse back into my backpack, getting rid of the most obvious evidence that I'd started all this. Then I began crawling on the floor too. I made my way to the middle of the room, squeezing past butts and getting jabbed by elbows as I headed toward Niles's bag.

"Why search for the treasure?" Mei asked. I peeked toward the front of the room, where Mei was still in her seat. "If Mrs. Hasan didn't set up the treasure hunt, the prize can't be anything good."

"Sure it could," argued someone from the far side of the room. "Mrs. Jones is the most likely person to have set up a prank involving the SMART board. She always fixes them when they're out of whack."

"I'd take ten points on a computer-science test or an excused homework in that class too," said someone else.

"I wouldn't," Mei said, crossing her arms. "I have art for my elective."

"Find the treasure and give it to me, and I'll be your best mate." That was Niles. He was all the way on the left side of the room, teaming up with Rick to search. He must not be doing well in computer programming, because he was looking under anything not affixed to the floor for the treasure.

"I certainly hope another teacher wouldn't have pranked my class!" Mrs. Hasan was back to fooling around with her mouse, trying to get the pointer to the reboot button, but of course, it wouldn't budge.

When I reached Niles's desk, I looked around. Niles was busy searching the front of the room. Time to dig through his bag!

I slid open the zipper and paged through notebooks and three-ring binders. I couldn't find anything that looked like tests. I even checked the notebook sitting on his desk, and duh, of course the tests wouldn't be anyplace out in the open. Finally, I checked the small front pocket of his bag. Nothing.

Now what was I going to do? I was so sure Niles had done it.

Sweat broke out on the back of my neck. There was only

another minute or two left in my program. It'd been hard to think up rhyming clues that sounded like they came from a pirate captain. I'd only come up with a handful.

I needed to figure this out fast.

I went through Niles's bag a second time, looking not specifically for the test, but just for anything that looked suspicious. Still, I came up empty.

I couldn't stay here, paging through Niles's stuff. Eventually, he'd notice or someone else would. I looked under the desk next to his to give me a minute to think. Should I search other bags? There were some other people from pre-algebra in this class. But who? Who was the next most likely suspect?

I'd just looked over at Mei when she read the second clue from the screen, getting the attention of everyone crawling around the floor: "'You'll walk the plank if you can't solve this caper, so look amid something made out of paper.'"

Mei scanned the room with a puzzled expression on her face, but Rick and Niles immediately darted to the bookshelves in the back of the room and started pulling down one title after another. Mei must have decided the treasure was worthwhile, because she was quick to follow.

I moved quickly as well—toward Rick's bag. I should have thought of him right away. Niles and Rick were best friends. If Niles needed help hiding something, Rick would be the first person he'd turn to. Plus, no one would ever think of searching his bag, because Rick wasn't in pre-algebra with us. While they rifled through the bookshelves at the back of the room, I rifled through Rick's bag, taking care to keep desks between them and me so they couldn't see what I was doing.

Again, there was nothing amid the notebooks and binders that looked like a class-worth of tests, but there had to be something here, and I had to find it. I couldn't believe I'd created this awesome prank and that it'd worked, disrupting the entire social studies class as a diversion, but I still couldn't find the tests.

Rick's bag had a ton of zippered compartments, a couple big ones and a bunch of smaller ones for pens, a calculator, or whatever. I searched every one. I'd made it to the smallest, least likely pocket when I found a note folded up into a neat, compact square. The words "DESTROY ME" were written across it in letters that were gouged into the paper, like someone had used a lot of force to write them.

I'd have rather found the tests, but this could be an important clue. I slid the note into my pocket and re-zipped every compartment in Rick's bag. Then I crawled away from Rick's desk to avoid drawing his or Niles's attention. But there was no need to worry. They were still pulling books off shelves.

Every student in the classroom was now frantically searching for treasure. Mrs. Hasan had her back to the mayhem. She was on the phone, asking someone for emergency SMART board help.

"Oh, for heaven's sake!" she exclaimed, slamming the phone down. "I'm going to get Mrs. Jones. Whether or not she planned this prank, she can stop it." She stomped out the door.

Knowing what the next clue was, I stood and stepped nimbly over the people still searching the "deck." I dodged classmates heading for the bookshelves at the back of the room to get to the SMART board.

I'd run out of time trying to figure out how a pirate would describe a SMART board. The technology didn't really translate into pirate lingo. I wanted to be the one to read the next clue to make sure everyone got it. "Look!" I said when the clue came up. "'Gold and silver are one type of treasure, but knowledge holds wealth in greater measure.'"

I let out a fake gasp before supplying the answer. "The SMART board! Knowledge in great measure is the SMART board because it's connected to the internet with access to all kinds of information."

My classmates bought my bad acting and crowded around the device. Other than checking behind the screen, there wasn't much to find around the SMART board. The mouse and keyboard still didn't work, so they couldn't search the hard drive. Everyone soon went back to checking underneath desks and around the books. I took that opportunity to remove my receiver and flash drive from the SMART board slots. I pulled Mrs. Hasan's receiver from my pocket and returned it to its proper slot.

While the rest of the class continued searching for clues, I went back to my seat, pulled the note out of my pocket, and flattened out the folds. I skimmed for incriminating evidence and my eyes latched onto key phrases.

Totally screwed up at the cinema . . .

. . . Coke all down her leg!

You'd have died laughing if you were there!

. . . felt like such an idiot!

I realized with a start that this note wasn't about stealing math tests at all. It was about Niles dumping Coke all over Trinidad in the movie theater last Friday! No wonder I'd gotten the feeling that things hadn't gone so well for him. I couldn't stifle a snort.

Unfortunately, Niles and Rick had given up on the books and were heading back toward their seats. My snort drew Niles's attention, and when he noticed the note in front of me, his face flushed bright red. He elbowed Rick.

Now I was really in trouble. I didn't have any evidence that he'd stolen the math tests, *and* I had an incredibly embarrassing personal note.

Chapter 11

Niles, 11:53 a.m.

My face flamed for what seemed like the millionth time today. I imagined it glowing red-hot like those bad guys in *Iron Man 3* just before they detonated, taking out a hundred square yards in all directions. *Why was today so monumentally embarrassing?*

Okay, the movie-and-Coke disaster was a problem left over from the weekend, but I'd had to face Trinidad today. She'd said it was no big deal, but she must think I am the biggest klutz in the entire school.

And just when I was about to suggest another group meet-up at the cinema to the girls, Amir butted in on our conversation and pulled that prank. He had Trinidad and Claudia both massively upset! Okay, the fake punch was not my best idea, but why was I getting all the blame when he had started everything with the fake wrist break?

Now he was sitting there with my private note, and he was *reading it. In class.* Where *anyone* could walk by and see!

I ripped the note from Amir's hand. "That's personal!"

Amir pulled back as far from me as his seat would allow, which wasn't very far. "Sorry! I thought you took the math tests. That's what I was looking for."

"Why would I steal the math tests?" That excuse was completely ridiculous. It only made me more frustrated.

"Why were you looking in *my* bag for them?" Rick was right next to me, also glaring down at Amir.

"Niles Shingleton and Rick Thomas, back off," Mrs. Jones said sternly as she marched into the room.

Mrs. Hasan hustled in behind her, sweating. "Take your seats, all of you."

I shot Amir one more hard look, muttering, "This is not over," before Rick and I both took our seats.

This time, I held on to the note. Obviously, Rick had not found a safe enough place for *private* information.

I wanted to light up the page with a match and watch it burn until it was completely destroyed. But doing that in the middle of a classroom would get me expelled, so instead I tore the note in half, then in half again. I ripped each of the remaining bits into scraps so tiny they couldn't hold more than one letter of the original message. Even if someone found all the pieces, they wouldn't be able to reassemble the note into anything readable.

When I finished shredding the note into confetti, I finally felt a bit better.

Meanwhile, the teachers were dealing with the SMART board. Mrs. Hasan waved at it. "These cat memes started appearing out of nowhere—zooming in from the side of the screen, spinning, exploding."

"Animated JPEG files." Mrs. Jones rubbed the back of her neck. "I would never disrupt another teacher's class, but I'm afraid I might have taught the culprit how to. We covered how to program things like this earlier this year. It's not hard."

"Maybe you need to discuss with your students the situations in which using computer-programming tricks is appropriate, *and when it is not*." Mrs. Hasan seemed to be directing the second half of that sentence more at the class than at Mrs. Jones.

I looked back at Amir again. He sat up straight, hands folded on his desk, eyes focused intently on the two teachers. He looked angelic. Of course he did. He didn't want to draw attention to himself. He was both a prankster *and* had one of the top grades in computer programming. He must have created the SMART board takeover program as a distraction so he could search for the tests. And I'd totally fallen for it. How could today get any worse?

But that still didn't explain why he thought I had taken the tests to begin with.

"I see we share a couple students between our classes." Mrs. Jones scanned the room, her gaze lingering on those of us who were in programming. "We'll discuss this eighth period."

I knew I hadn't messed with Mrs. Hasan's SMART board, but the look on the computer teacher's face still made me nauseous. Mrs. Jones looked ready to put us under a bright light and interrogate us like a government agent getting info out of a spy.

"I look forward to hearing the results of that discussion," Mrs. Hasan said. "But for now, I'm most interested in how I can get my presentation back up without harming the SMART board."

"Well, if you can shut down the system—" Mrs. Jones's hand went to the mouse.

"The mouse doesn't work—"

Before Mrs. Hasan even got the words out of her mouth, it became clear that they weren't true. Mrs. Jones was easily able to use the mouse to bring the pointer down to the restart button to reboot the system.

Mrs. Hasan pushed her glasses higher on the bridge of her nose. She blinked a couple times. "That mouse didn't work just minutes ago."

"So there's no treasure?" Mei asked.

"Just a week's detention for our computer hacker," Mrs. Hasan said.

Excellent! Five of Amir's afternoons were now in the palm of my hand. All I had to do was mention he'd been searching bags to prove he'd been the one who had hacked the computer. But that would bring up my note. My stomach flipped again. I'd just destroyed it, and even though I could still provide the pile of confetti on my desk as proof it existed, I didn't want the topic in the note to come up at all. How could I turn Amir in without bringing up Coke-drenched jeans?

I sat there stewing over that dilemma while we all listened to the hard drive crank and hum to bring itself back to the state in which we'd started class, with just Civil War battles, not cat memes, on the screen. When the home screen came up with Harwington Middle School's name and logo, Mrs. Hasan let out an enormous sigh of relief.

"Thank you, Gloria! I can finally get on with today's curriculum."

"You're welcome," Mrs. Jones said. "I'm sorry my coursework was used to disrupt your class, and I'm looking forward to an interesting discussion in eighth period."

Amir, you're in big trouble, mate. Even if I couldn't turn him in, there were only a handful of us in both classes. He'd get caught.

After Mrs. Jones left, class was uneventful, if a bit rushed because of how much time we'd lost to cat memes. I took the notes I'd need to study for the test, but mostly, my mind was on Amir. I wanted to know why he thought I had taken the math tests and why he had been reading my private notes.

When the bell rang, I squeezed through the aisles to the door to make sure Amir couldn't disappear. When Amir reached the hallway, Rick and I stuck like glue to either side of him.

"Why were you going through Rick's things?" I asked.

Amir hunched a bit under my glare. "Sorry, my bad! Like I said, I saw the note and figured it was about the pre-algebra tests."

"It wasn't!" I said.

He rolled his eyes. "I get that now, but Trinidad says Miss Palermo's in big trouble for losing the tests. She asked me to help find them."

"Trinidad thinks I stole the tests?"

Amir shrugged. "You were quiet in homeroom. You're *never* quiet in homeroom. Plus, you wanted to get out of math to 'help' Miss Palermo. I thought it was because you didn't want to get caught with the tests."

"You were trying to get out of the classroom too," Rick said.

"Yeah, that's why Trinidad pulled me into this to begin with. She thought I wanted to stash the tests in Miss Palermo's car as an April Fools' joke."

"You didn't, but you still thought the same thing about me?"

Amir waved his hands. "It seemed to make sense at the time."

We continued walking down the hall in silence, despite the loud conversations around us. My mind whirred. Trinidad was trying to get Miss Palermo's tests back.

"You didn't answer my question. Did you think I stole the tests, or does Trinidad think that?" If she did, I had a much bigger problem than that note and the fact that Amir had read it. If she thought I'd stolen the math tests and gotten her favorite teacher in trouble, she'd never go out with me.

"No. She thought I took them as a prank. *I* thought it was you."

"Not surprising Trinidad thought of you," Rick said. "You're known for pulling pranks, even on Miss Palermo."

Amir squeezed around a group of girls bunched at an open locker before he answered. "She has a better sense of humor than most of our teachers. It lowers the likelihood I'll end up in detention. Also, that dried-glue-on-keyboard prank was stellar. She totally thought milk was about to ruin her keyboard."

"Let's focus!" I slapped one hand across the other to get their attention. "We have a situation here. Trinidad wants to find those tests for Miss Palermo. We're going to help her."

"How?" asked Rick. "We have no idea who took those tests."

I stopped in the middle of the hall, forcing Rick and Amir to stop as well, so they'd really listen. "Actually, we do. I saw Mei tailing Trinidad and Claudia down the hall right after pre-algebra."

"What does that have to do with anything?" Amir asked.

"I also caught her trying to break into Trinidad's locker in the middle of second period," I said. "When I walked by, she pretended she'd stopped at the wrong locker. But I watched her from around the corner. She went right back to Trinidad's locker."

Rick's eyebrows went up. "Okay, that sounds more suspicious."

Amir's face crinkled up. "I don't know. Mei's usually quoting rules, not breaking them."

"True," Rick said. "It's kind of annoying, actually."

My last piece of evidence would leave no room for doubt. "Have you noticed how frigid things have gotten between them since the lacrosse season started? Mei's furious that Trinidad is playing center attack."

"Ah," Rick and Amir both said, and we started toward the lunchroom again.

"I didn't see Mei get the locker open, but what if she tried again later? She might have stashed the tests in Trinidad's locker to make her look guilty. Why else would she have been in that hallway in the middle of class?"

Amir's brow wrinkled up as he tried to come up with an explanation, but in the end, he just shrugged.

"So you're going to try and prove Mei took the math tests so that you can get another shot at a date with Trinidad?" Rick asked.

"No, *we're* going to prove Mei took the tests." But if that got me a chance at another date, I certainly wouldn't turn it down.

"Count me out," Amir said, turning to head down a different hallway.

"Oh no." I slid my arm around his shoulder in a friendly yet you're-not-going-anywhere gesture. "You owe me for stealing and reading that note, and I'm collecting."

Chapter 12

Niles, 12:20 p.m.

"Gotta study for a programming quiz!" I called to friends at my usual lunch table as I walked past them. Rick, Amir, and I snagged the empty end of a table at the back of the cafeteria to hash out a plan for attacking the missing math test problem.

"What's your idea?" Amir asked as he got out his lunch.

He opened a thermos with some fragrant tea. It definitely wasn't the Earl Grey that my mom drank. He'd heated up two containers in one of the school's microwave ovens. One held rice.

The other contained some kind of green stew that he spooned over the rice. What was that stuff?

"I went through your bag hoping you still had the tests on you," Amir continued. "When I didn't find them, I tried Rick's bag. But *if* Mei took the tests and *if* she stashed them in Trinidad's locker, we're out of luck."

Amir scooped up a spoonful of rice and stew. Now the scent hit me, and I had to admit, it made my mouth water. Garlic and chicken and something I couldn't place. Normally, toad in the hole was my favorite lunch, but today, it just wasn't measuring up.

"Let's use that SMART board prank again," I said. "We'll change it up so it doesn't look the same, make it creepy—full of ghosts and spooks, rather than cat memes. If the ghost behind the SMART board accuses Mei of taking the tests, she'll panic and admit she did it."

"Won't work," Rick said between bites of a lunchroom hot dog so loaded down with ketchup and mustard you could hardly see the meat. "She already saw that trick in social studies."

"She doesn't know Amir was behind it," I said.

"She knows," Amir said. "She's been avoiding my pranks since before classes started this morning. She'd suspect me of being behind any gag pulled in this school."

"Hmm. That's a problem." I didn't want Trinidad to get blamed for stealing those tests, and if they were found in her locker, she would be. That'd mess up her application to that STEM school she wanted to go to. I had to admit, I'd rather she was at Harwington High with the rest of us next year, but I wasn't going to let Mei ruin Trinidad's shot at her dream school just because of that.

"There's got to be something we can do." I stabbed another sausage and chewed it while I thought.

Rick shrugged. Amir ate some more green stuff and rice. His leg jiggled under the table, making it and all our food wobble a bit.

"Don't you have any more great pranks, Amir?"

He shook his head.

"What if . . .," Rick started. Then his shoulders slumped. "No, that won't work." He took another huge bite of hot dog.

"What won't work?" I asked. "We're desperate for ideas here."

Rick swallowed the enormous bite. I watched the lump slide down his throat.

"I was just thinking about science," he said. "Mr. Gopal asked Mei to feed Rattatat, and she was creeped out. Why? All you need to do is drop a bit of food into his bowl. You don't even have to touch him if you don't want to."

"Why wouldn't you want to touch him?" Amir asked. "He's cute and totally tame."

"Sure," Rick said. "I'm just saying that Mei was freaked. Maybe she's seen too many horror movies with thousands of rats scurrying out of sewers and attacking everyone."

"Rattatat . . ." That got me thinking. "What if we tied a message around his neck? 'Give back the tests or else, Mei.' And see what she does."

Rick scrunched up his face. "Then what? We just deposit Rattatat with this note in her lap?" He looked across the cafeteria to where Mei sat with a couple girls from the lacrosse team.

"I'm still working out the details, okay?" I grumbled. "Also, don't look. She'll know we're up to something!"

Rick turned back, taking another huge bite of hot dog. The whole thing was gone in three bites, except for the ketchup coating his fingers.

"Amir and I will sort out how the Rattatat part of the plan plays out," I said. "Meanwhile, someone needs to catch Trinidad before seventh period and have her check her locker for the math tests. She needs to turn them in so Mei can't lead a teacher there to find them. That's your job, Rick."

"I want that job," Amir said. "That job sounds like it won't get me in more trouble than I'm already in for pranks today."

"Those cat memes were awesome," Rick said. "Even if they get you in trouble in social studies, they should get you extra credit in computer programming."

"Mrs. Jones didn't look too happy." Amir scraped the last of the green stuff onto his spoon and ate it, clearly relishing the taste.

"What is that?" I asked.

Amir swallowed before answering. "Ghormeh sabzi."

"Never heard of it."

"It's a spicy stew made with herbs, beans, and chicken cubes. My mom made a huge pot this weekend. Tomorrow, I'll bring some for you to try." Amir gestured at my now-empty lunch container. "What were you eating?"

"You've never had toad in the hole? It's sausages in pudding."

Amir looked a little dubious. "That didn't look like any kind of pudding I've ever had."

I shook my head. "Not Jell-O type pudding. *Real* pudding. I'll bring some tomorrow too. But, hey, do you have any of those plastic cups left from this morning?"

Amir unzipped the backpack sitting next to him on the bench. He still had a couple dozen plastic cups. How many times did he think he could fake-break his wrist in one day?

"Did Mr. Gopal see your prank this morning?" I asked. He was the teacher on lunch duty today.

Amir shook his head. "Why?"

"While Rick's talking to Trinidad, we need an excuse to break out of here and get Rattatat."

"I still think talking to Trinidad is the part of this plan least likely to get me in trouble," Amir said. "Are we even if I help with this?"

"We're even if you help *and* never tell Trinidad about the note," I said.

"Deal." Amir held out his hand. I shook it.

He pulled one of the cups out of his bag and stuck it up under his armpit, then tugged his jacket over it, hiding the cup completely. "One broken wrist coming up."

Chapter 13

Niles, 12:35 p.m.

Amir delivered a brilliant performance on the wrist-break prank.
I appreciated it much more now that it was getting me an escape
from the lunchroom, rather than making Trinidad mad at me.
Mr. Gopal, who'd been walking by our table, panicked.

"I'll walk him to Nurse Travers!" I volunteered before the
teacher could drag Amir out the door himself.

Mr. Gopal waved us out of the lunchroom with a "Keep it
elevated! I'll call to let her know you're coming!"

We took off. Even if Mr. Gopal hadn't seen that prank this morning, there were plenty of people in that room who had. Someone was sure to tell him, and we needed to be gone before they did.

I headed straight for the science classroom at the fastest pace I could without looking suspicious. Amir followed.

"I know you don't want to get into any more trouble, Amir. You don't have to help me."

"I might as well," Amir said. "I can't really go to the nurse's office. She'd figure out pretty quick my wrist isn't actually broken."

That reminded me that Amir had agreed to pull that prank knowing it would catch up with him. Really, he was a pretty good guy. I wondered why I'd never gotten to know him better. Maybe we'd keep eating lunch together after we swapped food tomorrow.

"Thanks," I said.

He nodded, and we continued down the hall.

When we got to the empty science classroom, Amir found a box to carry Rattatat in while I wrote the note and tried to tie it around the rat's neck. I was lucky I had Amir's help. Rattatat wasn't asleep for once, and he was not excited about having a message attached to him. He twisted in my hands, his furry body making him hard to hold on to. I wouldn't have made it to Spanish in time to hide the box under Mei's seat if Amir hadn't pitched in.

Since he did, we were the first students to reach Miss Mendosa's room, arriving just as the first bell rang.

"How do we get Rattatat in without her noticing?" Amir asked.

"The key is to look confident. Chin up, shoulders back. My dad always says 90 percent of confidence is posture."

As I said the words, Amir stood straighter. He looked about two inches taller than normal. "Does your dad have any more advice for this situation?"

I winced. "I don't think so."

"Well, I'll go in first. Keep the box behind me so Miss Mendosa can't see it."

"Good plan."

The Spanish teacher looked up from the papers she was grading long enough to say, "Hello, boys," then turned back to her work. That was all we needed.

I slid Rattatat's box under Mei's seat, then Amir and I both sat down. I tried to take my own advice, sit with a straight spine, and pretend everything was normal. But as the minutes dragged on, I thought of things that could go wrong with this plan.

"Amir!" I muttered in a low voice.

His seat was near the door. When he turned, I waved him over.

"What if he doesn't chew his way out of the box and Mei never sees him?" I asked.

Amir's eyes went wide, but then he said, "Hold on." He ran back to his seat and pulled something out of his bag.

When he got back, I saw what it was. "Rice."

"I had a little left over from lunch. Rattatat should love it, right?" he asked. "It smells much better than the pellets we usually feed him."

"Great idea!"

Mei's seat was in the middle of the room, between mine and Amir's. Amir checked to make sure Miss Mendosa was still focused on the quizzes, then he dropped the rice next to Rattatat's box and started back toward his seat.

"Wait," I called in a low voice.

Amir came back.

"What if Rattatat can't smell it? He's pretty old."

Amir's brow furrowed. "Or it'll take him the rest of the school day and half the night to gnaw his way out of the box."

"Then we're sunk."

"I'll make a little hole in one corner. That'll solve both problems. He'll smell the snack and have a head start breaking out."

Amir crouched down and fooled around with the box for a few seconds. He was up and taking his seat just as our classmates began to arrive. Mei walked in, still chatting up the lacrosse friends she ate lunch with. She never looked under her desk. Her feet almost touched the box.

A minute later, Rick arrived with Trinidad and Claudia. Trinidad waved at me, and the girls took their seats at the front of the room while Rick took his seat next to me.

He leaned over. "No sign of the tests. Hope your plan for getting info out of Mei works."

"Me, too, mate. Otherwise, our plan is gutted."

"Speaking of the plan, I didn't tell Trinidad about part two," Rick said.

"Why not?"

"Plausible deniability, just in case everything goes wrong."

"Thanks for your vote of confidence," I said dryly. Still, I had to admit that fewer people knowing I was behind a rat let loose in the classroom was better.

The room filled up. Miss Mendosa had just started class when our furry friend made his presence known. The first thing I noticed was his little pink nose poking out of the small hole in the box. No one else spotted him. No one else had their eyes glued to the floor, rather than the teacher. I imagined the little guy sniffing for food.

The box wriggled as Rattatat worked at the cardboard, but if that made any noise, I couldn't hear it over the discussion of last night's homework.

More of Rattatat's pink nose became visible, then a tiny claw. The hole still seemed way too small for him to fit through when he squirmed his body halfway out and someone screamed.

"Mei, there's a rat under your desk!"

Mei simultaneously pulled her feet up off the floor and swung her body to one side to look beneath her desk. She screamed, too, then jumped up on her chair, almost toppling it over in her rush to put space between herself and the rodent.

"Did you say a *rat*? How could a rat get into my classroom?" Miss Mendosa shifted one way, then the other, trying to see around students and desks.

Rattatat, clueless about the hysteria he was creating, nibbled at the rice.

"Quick! Somebody catch it!" called Claudia, but everyone either pulled up their feet or stood on their chairs like Mei. They didn't want any body parts close to a rat.

"I've got this!" Trinidad jumped out of her seat, her heavy three-ring binder in her hands. She slowly stalked over to Mei's desk. "Come out, come out, little guy," she said in a singsongy voice.

My heart leapt to my throat. "What're you gonna do?"

"Smash it!" Trinidad yelled.

"Don't!" Amir leapt to save Rattatat.

I ran to the rat's rescue too. I couldn't let Trinidad

unknowingly smash Rattatat! If she showed up to science tomorrow and realized she'd killed the class pet, she'd never forgive herself. Or me.

It turned out Rattatat didn't need our help. He dashed across the classroom faster than I'd ever seen him move. I couldn't see his small, caramel-colored body as he slid under desks, but my classmates' squeals and shrieks gave me a pretty accurate picture of his location. Trinidad, Amir, and I took off after him, dodging desks and each other as we went.

"I'll defend the exit." Claudia planted herself by the door to make sure the rat couldn't get away.

"What if we just trap it under something?" Miss Mendosa suggested, but she didn't move to find a trap. Instead, she jumped up on her desk chair.

"Yes, trap him, don't smash him," Amir agreed.

He got down on one side of the desk Rattatat was hiding under. I got down on the other side. Trinidad hovered nearby, holding the binder over her shoulder with two hands like it was her lacrosse stick and she was about to hurl the winning goal into the net.

The owner of the desk wriggled, threatening to tip over her seat. "Just get it away from me!"

"Don't worry! I'll get help from the front office." Miss Mendosa frantically punched numbers on the classroom phone.

I had to keep myself between Trinidad and Rattatat. Meanwhile, the whole point of this prank was to get a confession out of Mei, and so far, we had nothing. I wasn't sure if she'd even noticed the note around his neck.

"Sorry, Rattatat," I whispered. Then I called out, "Look! The rat has a message. 'Give back the tests or else, Mei.' "

I swatted at poor Rattatat, and he scurried across the room toward the test thief. I worried that the poor little guy might faint from the extreme level of exercise he was enduring today, but it'd take something more than just reading the message to get Mei to spill the beans. I hoped one more pass would get the job done.

Mei shrieked again, her eyes on Rattatat as he streaked back her way. "I didn't take the tests! Why does the rat think I took the tests? Trinidad took them! She's the one who messed up Friday's test and wanted to retake it to get a better grade!"

"What?" Trinidad's gaze went from the rodent to Mei. "I didn't take them! I was trying to find them to get Miss Palermo out of trouble. Amir took them. It was his April Fools' prank." She shot Amir a harsh glare, then apparently remembered she was trying to smash a rat and sprinted across the room.

"I didn't do it, even though it would have been a pretty good prank!" Amir shouted. He kept trying to protect Rattatat from Trinidad even while he defended himself. "I thought Niles took the tests, because he was oddly quiet in math this morning but, well . . ."

"I didn't take them—I was just embarrassed about dousing Trinidad's jeans with Coke at the cinema!" I called out as I hopped over an empty desk to beat Trinidad to Rattatat.

I'd spent all day trying to keep the news about my blunder under wraps. But now, with Rattatat running for his life, Trinidad trying to smash him, and the math tests still missing, I figured looking like a dunce was the least of my problems.

I pressed Mei again. "I saw you trying to break into Trinidad's locker in the middle of second period. What were you doing there if you weren't trying to frame Trinidad?"

Mei's eyes were on the floor next to her desk where Rattatat was trying to make his way back into the box we'd carried him in to hide. "I was trying to get the tests back from Trinidad!" she screeched.

"What on earth is going on in here?"

Principal Alvero and Miss Palermo stuck their heads into the classroom, craning their necks to see around Claudia just as Trinidad and I reached Mei's desk. We collided in our rush to be the first to Rattatat and knocked into Mei's desk as we crashed to the floor. I was pinned down with Trinidad half on top of me, our arms and legs tangled up. My face was probably Coke-can red from sprinting across the room, so at this point the extra flush from Trinidad's face landing pretty much in my armpit hardly mattered.

Meanwhile, the desk rocked, sending Mei flying into Amir. They crashed to the floor on the other side of the desk.

Since I was down at Rattatat's level, I checked his box.

Empty.

Then I scanned beneath the nearby desks.

I spotted him. He was under the desk in front of Mei's, just out of my reach. Luckily, he was out of Trinidad's reach too.

Rattatat took off again, this time making a break for the open space and relative quiet of the hallway.

"Oh no!" I moaned. "Don't let Rattatat get away!"

Claudia dove for the rat, but missed. He scuttled by her. Then, with one fell swoop, Miss Palermo dumped the crunched-up papers and snack wrappers from the waste bin by the door and brought the bin over Rattatat, preventing his escape.

Principal Alvero straightened his tie, got his serious face on, and said, "Miss Mendosa, I'll need to speak with a few of your students in my office. Now."

Chapter 14

Monday, April 1, 1:05 p.m.

"Are you all okay?" Miss Palermo asked as we trudged down the hall toward Principal Alvero's office. Principal Alvero had called out five names to come with him: Mei, Amir, Trinidad, Niles, and Claudia. Rick, slumped down in his seat at the back of the classroom, had escaped.

Amir assured her that he was fine. Mei huffed indignantly and ran her fingers through her long black hair to get it back in place.

"Sorry," Niles said to Trinidad, who rubbed her elbow as she walked. She'd jabbed him in the head with it on her way down.

"I'm all right. I landed on you, though. Are you okay?"

"Sure," Niles said, though it wasn't really the truth. Her elbow was pretty sharp, and his head ached. Niles rubbed the spot, but he could hardly feel sorry for himself. He'd put Rattatat through the scare of his short rodent life. He'd never imagined it'd be so hard to spook the truth out of Mei. And he was gutted that they hadn't found the tests or figured out who'd swiped them.

When they reached the office, Principal Alvero sat behind his desk and let the full weight of his disapproval show in his frown. "April Fools' Day is always a little chaotic, but with these missing pre-algebra tests, things have gotten way out of hand."

Mei folded her arms over her chest and scowled. "I can't give back tests I don't have."

Amir collapsed into one of the chairs in front of the principal's desk, exhausted enough from the day's events to risk the "bad kid" seat. "I really can't face *another* math test tomorrow."

"You won't have to, Amir. None of you will." Miss Palermo brushed the blue streak of hair out of her face. "I have the math tests. I never lost them."

"Seriously?" Amir jumped right back out of the chair. The news about the tests was almost too good to be true.

"I can't believe it!" Trinidad felt the stress fall from her shoulders. She had spent the whole day worried about Miss Palermo getting in trouble over the tests.

"But teachers don't pull pranks!" exclaimed Mei. Her mother was *so* going to hear about this. The only thing that could possibly be worse than a teacher losing the tests for an entire class was a teacher *not* losing the tests and pretending she had. Mei hadn't been able to find a rule banning students from pulling pranks at school, but there must be a rule against teachers pulling pranks.

"I'm sorry." Miss Palermo perched on the edge of Principal Alvero's desk, looking tired. "All I can say is that I never thought you'd be so upset about retaking the test, Amir. Or anyone else. Everyone seemed to like Amir's pranks so much, especially that milk-covered keyboard one. It had me panicked for a minute, but when I realized what you'd done, I thought it was so clever and creative. I was inspired to try a prank myself.

"I thought I'd give everyone a good laugh when I announced, 'April Fools'!' over the loudspeaker at the end of the day today, and you'd be happy when I said there was no homework. But my test prank got everyone too riled up. I never imagined you'd break into each other's lockers, disrupt classes, or let rats loose to figure out who stole the tests."

"Miss Palermo came to me earlier today, but I thought giving the prank some time to play out would be a good learning experience. Has anyone learned something from the missing-test prank?" Principal Alvero met the eyes of each of the students in turn, hitting them with a penetrating stare that made it seem like he was reading their minds. No one dared speak.

Mei finally raised a hand after a long moment. "I learned

that there are no rules against pranks in the Student Code of Conduct. There should be. And in the teachers' rule book too."

Amir looked horrified at this idea. "But pranks are fun!"

"Not to the people who panic when they think your wrist is broken," Trinidad said. "Sorry," she added when she saw his disappointment.

Amir screwed up his face. "Actually, I get that now. Thinking I'd have to retake the math test wasn't at all fun. You totally had me fooled, Miss Palermo." He held out a fist for the teacher to bump. She deserved props; he hadn't even suspected she was the "thief."

Miss Palermo bumped his fist and grinned.

"Why did you think Trinidad took the tests, Mei?" Principal Alvero asked.

"I had evidence. I heard her and Claudia talking about the fact that they hadn't studied enough and were happy to get a second shot at the test. That didn't seem fair."

But that wasn't all of it. She could see now that her lacrosse ambitions had made her jump to conclusions. "Also, I thought if I caught Trinidad with the stolen tests, she'd get in trouble and I'd get the starting position as center attacker on the lacrosse team."

"I didn't know you felt that strongly about playing attack, Mei," Miss Palermo said. "I thought you'd prefer defense because you tend to hang back, not play as aggressively as you could."

"I just don't want to get caught offsides. That's breaking the rules." Mei narrowed her eyes accusingly at Trinidad.

Trinidad made no apologies for playing aggressively. "If you don't push the rules a bit, you're not doing your job as attacker. It's kind of in the name of the position. You need to *attack* the ball. If you get caught offsides occasionally . . ." She shrugged. "That's part of the game. You pay for it with a turnover to make things fair."

Mei suddenly saw the way Trinidad played quite differently than she had before. "Is that why you've been putting me on defense, Miss Palermo? Because I'm too worried about the rules?"

"In some situations, obeying rules to the letter is important, but on the lacrosse field, you need to be more concerned about getting the ball up the field and into the net," the teacher said. "If you want to start as attacker, you need to be more aggressive."

Mei nodded. "I'm sorry I thought you were cheating at lacrosse, Trinidad. Also, that I thought you stole the tests."

"No problem," Trinidad said. "I learned something today too—that just because you're great at pulling pranks doesn't mean you pulled the biggest one of April Fools' Day. I'm sorry I thought you stole the tests, Amir."

"Me too," Claudia added.

Amir smiled. Claudia was talking to him. Claudia *hardly ever* talked to him, except when she'd accused him of stealing the tests. Amir channeled his inner Niles and stood tall. He needed all the confidence he could summon right now.

"You could make it up to me by not backing out on the movies on Saturday." Amir said this so fast the words ran together.

When Claudia caught his meaning, the tips of her ears turned pink with embarrassment. "There's a good comedy opening this weekend."

Amir nodded. "I'm dying to see it!"

Principal Alvero tapped his desk to get attention back on "learnings," rather than the weekend movie plans. "Did you learn anything today, Amir?"

"I learned that even guys with perfect hair and a seemingly perfect life can get embarrassed." Amir looked at Niles. He was a pretty good guy if you looked past the puffed-up chest and the walk that made him look like he was running for president or something.

"I don't know about perfect hair, especially after crawling around on the floor to protect Rattatat," Niles said. It was a good thing it was close to the end of the school day. He probably needed hair gel pretty badly at this point.

A shiver ran down Trinidad's spine. "I can't believe I was trying to squash our science pet!"

"Don't worry," Niles said. "I wouldn't have let you hurt him."

"Thank goodness!" Trinidad said. "By the way, do you like

comedies?" It was totally embarrassing to ask a guy out in the middle of the principal's office, but Amir had just asked Claudia . . .

"Is that an invitation?" Niles asked.

Trinidad smiled, and that was all the invitation Niles needed. "I'll be there. No bladder buster full of Coke this time."

Trinidad's smile broadened, lighting up her whole face. Niles couldn't wait for Saturday.

Principal Alvero rolled his eyes and tried again to gain control of the discussion. "Learnings . . .," he prompted.

"I learned that help can come from unexpected places." Niles slapped Amir on the shoulder. "Thanks for helping me out today."

"What *exactly* did Amir help you with?" Principal Alvero raised one eyebrow.

Amir winced, and Niles realized he needed to tread carefully to make sure this was a thank-you and not something that would get his new friend into more trouble.

"He helped me get over my Coke-spill fiasco. He also helped me get clear of the lunchroom so I could get Rattatat's help, but that prank was all on me. I asked him to do it." Niles figured he owed it to Amir to take all the blame for the Rattatat incident. Maybe if Mrs. Jones didn't figure out Amir had pulled the SMART board prank in social studies, he wouldn't catch too much heat.

Principal Alvero waited, as if he knew that the class's biggest prankster had helped with more than that. When Niles remained silent, he said, "I'm pretty sure we've all learned not to make assumptions."

"Yes, Principal Alvero," all of the students said.

"And I've learned that tests are not a good subject for pranks," Miss Palermo said. "I guarantee that I will not be 'misplacing' any math tests for the rest of the school year." She gave the students a sheepish smile. "Speaking of tests . . . I've got them to pass back."

Miss Palermo pulled the folder full of tests that had been "missing" all day from the bag she'd been carrying. "Trinidad."

Trinidad winced as she stepped forward to take the test. "An 85! I knew I'd messed up." She flipped from one page to the next, checking what she'd gotten wrong.

"I'll trade you that 85 for whatever I got," Claudia said just as she received her test from Miss Palermo. "A 79.5. That rounds to 80!" Claudia grinned.

Trinidad gave her a high five.

"Extra math help is available every day before school and after school on days we don't have lacrosse," Miss Palermo said. "You could get that grade up a bit, Claudia."

Handing Amir his test, she added in a lower voice, "I suggest you take me up on that offer too."

Amir looked at the grade on the math test she handed him. "That's not as bad as I thought it'd be, but I'll come by anyway."

When Mei received her grade, she said, "An 85! I was sure I aced this test!" She stuffed the test in her bag. "If I'd known I had gotten an 85, I'd have been okay with retaking it."

"And Niles." Miss Palermo handed Niles his test.

He knew even before looking at the grade that he should get extra math help with his new friend.

When all the tests were passed back, Miss Palermo said, "I'm glad we've got a year to recover before we have to face April Fools' Day again."

Principal Alvero scratched his head. "I think I need to warn the high school principal about the trouble we're sending her way in September."

As the students walked back to class, Mei eyed her classmates. "Please tell me we've learned our lesson and are not going to pull April Fools' pranks in high school."

Amir grinned mischievously.

"We've learned not to stage tricks that will get people super worried," Trinidad said. "But I think there's still some room for fun. I heard about cat memes taking over Mrs. Hasan's SMART board. I'm sure there are some useful prank skills I can learn at the STEM school next year."

"We can come up with a tech gag and use it at both Harwington High and the magnet school," Niles said. "Double trouble!"

Amir turned to Mei. "Are you in? You need some practice learning to bend the rules."

Mei tossed her hair over her shoulder. "Well, someone's got to keep an eye on you guys."

"If we start planning now," Trinidad said, "next year's prank will be truly epic!"

About the Author

Rebecca J. Allen grew up with her nose stuck in magical stories like *A Wrinkle in Time* and *The Hobbit*, where characters living in wondrous worlds seemed to learn and grow just the way they needed to in order the save the day. She rediscovered her love of magical books while reading to her kids. Now, she writes middle grade stories that blend mystery and adventure and young adult stories with heroines much braver than she is. You can find her at RebeccaJAllen.com. She's also on Twitter and Instagram as @ RebeccaJ_Allen.

About the Illustrator

Courtney Huddleston lives in Houston, Texas, with his wife, two daughters, and two cats named Lilo and Stitch. When he's not in his home studio working, he can usually be found playing video games, drooling over the work of other artists, going on long walks, or playing pranks on the family. While he gets inspiration from everything around him, his favorite way to get inspired is through travel. Courtney has been to most of the states in the United States, and he has visited more than a dozen other countries. He is currently searching for less expensive inspirations.